Always Her Cowboy

Always Her Cowboy

Search for Love Series

KAREN ROSE SMITH

To My Readers

I began writing seriously about twenty five years ago after back surgery. I was flat on my back for four years and needed something more creative than crocheting! I had been an English teacher so the mechanics of writing came easily. I'd read romances since I was a teenager and had always been fascinated by relationships so writing romance seemed natural, too. I started with short stories but when they were too long to market, I decided I should just write a book. I wrote for six years and completed thirteen manuscripts before I was bought. Then I sold two manuscripts to two different publishing houses within a week.

Since then, I've written over 80 novels. My main themes usually revolve around the healing power of love and family. The main theme of Always Her Cowboy is that we can't escape the pain of living. But love, of a family or of a significant other, can heal past hurts as well as teach us about new joy.

Western settings are my favorite. The expansive scenery generates beautiful images. When I visited Wyoming where ALWAYS HER COWBOY is set, we spotted wild mustangs in The Big Horns, visited Yellowstone, and enjoyed a rodeo in Cody. I think you'll feel my love of this setting in this novel.

ALWAYS HER COWBOY is book 4 in my Search For Love series. I have recently released book 7, HER SISTER, which is contemporary women's fiction with mystery and romance. My career has branched out into mysteries and I enjoy weaving them into my romances.

My favorite past times include spending time with family and friends, caring for our three rescue cats, gardening and cooking. I think you'll find a taste of all of these in my books. I like to hear from my readers. You can email me through my websites at www.karenrosesmith.com and www.karenrosesmithmysteries.com.

Always Her Cowboy

Chapter One

When Lucy McIntyre heard the roar of a motorcycle breaking the solitude of the Rising Star Ranch, she went to the kitchen window and pushed back the lace curtain with its ivy pattern. The man on the Harley brought the machine to a halt at the path to the house. She watched him climb off, hang his helmet on the handlebar, and stand with his hands jammed into the back pockets of his jeans as he studied the barn, corrals, indoor arena, and outbuildings. Then his attention turned toward the porch that wound around the house. Although she'd expected someone by the name of Zackary Burke to apply for the job of temporary hand, she'd never expected him to look like this!

He wore boots and jeans, typical attire for men living in and around Long Brush, Wyoming. But the black leather jacket and the motorcycle told her he was from another place. His midnight hair—thick, wavy and unruly—needed a trim. He stood over six feet. She could tell even from here. With his broad shoulders and slim hips, all he needed was a Stetson and a horse to make him look as if he belonged.

Lucy didn't think she moved, but the man's eyes met hers through the window. Caught, embarrassed and mesmerized by something in the man's demeanor and gaze, every question she'd prepared for their interview vanished from her head.

Without any warning, he winked, gave her half a smile and started up the walk.

Flustered and determined not to be, Lucy crossed the kitchen, willing the heat in her cheeks to subside. But when she opened the door, the man was even taller and more powerfully masculine than he'd looked twenty feet away! The curiosity and male appraisal as his blue eyes drifted from her long brown hair to her boots brought even more heat to her cheeks and a dryness to her throat.

The man extended his hand. "Zack Burke. I saw the job notice at the feed store in Long Brush and talked with Tom McIntyre about it at the day before yesterday."

Lucy shook his hand, surprised by the heat of his skin, its rough texture and the sparks that zipped up her arm. "Tom McIntyre is my father." A McIntyre by name rather than birth, it had never seemed to matter because she'd never doubted that her adoptive parents loved her or that her older brothers accepted her. Always grateful for that love and acceptance, she knew without it, her life might have been much different.

"Is your father around?" Zack Burke asked with a lift of a black brow.

"Dad and my brother are mending fence. I'm going to talk with you a little more to see if we should hire you. This is a family-run ranch so family is involved in everything." She motioned toward the kitchen table.

Unzipping his jacket, Zack waited for Lucy to sit before he pulled out a chair at the large pine table. His knee brushed hers and he nonchalantly shifted in the high-backed chair with that half-smile back on his lips. "Your father told me how much the job pays, including room and board. He said it's temporary—until your brother gets back on his feet. But if he's out mending fence…"

"That's my older brother, Rick. You'd be standing in for my other brother, Marty. He…hasn't been himself lately. Too unreliable to depend on. With winter setting in soon, we need a reliable, all-around hand. We tend some cattle, but our main focus is our Quarter Horses. Dad's family has raised them for generations."

"If you check the references I gave your dad, you'll see I know how to ride, can cut calves, and I'm handy with a hammer."

Along with her father's estimation of the man after his phone conversation with him and inquiring about him at the boarding house in Long Brush where he'd been staying, her dad had given her Zackary Burke's references and she'd called all three of them. Zack's last temporary job had been on a ranch in southern Wyoming and the two before that on spreads in Colorado. His former employers had answered all her questions and agreed he was hard-working and dependable. But Lucy wanted to interview him herself, to rely on her own instincts for one very important reason.

"Why do you want this job, Mr. Burke?"

"Zack," he suggested with a full smile that was meant to disarm her completely. It almost did.

But she had learned her lesson about charm and appearances, and a man's definition of a woman. If this man didn't want her to stand on formality, she wouldn't, but she would get the answers she needed. "All right…Zack. Why do you want to work on the Rising Star?"

Giving a casual shrug, his gaze met hers. "When I like a place, I stop and work. Wyoming has enough wide spaces that a man can breathe, move around and not feel trapped."

Lucy felt a sudden fascination to know more about Zackary Burke and why he felt trapped. The light in his intense blue eyes had changed. The devil-may-care sparkle had disappeared and was replaced by shadows.

Knowing she was maybe probing where she shouldn't, she asked, "Why don't you stay anywhere more than a few months?"

His strongly chiseled jaw tightened. "I suspect you know how life on a ranch changes with the seasons. When the work's finished, I move on."

"But…"

"Miss McIntyre," he drawled. Again he gave her that nonchalant smile that showed her how mobile his lips could be and made her wonder how he kissed. The thought shocked her! Well, not the thought, but *her* having it.

"I like to travel," he continued. "Working like this, I've seen more of the United States than most people can only dream of seeing. And I like ranches—the miles of fence, the pine and larch, the bunkhouses where no one cares where you came from or where you're going."

If that was a subtle hint for her to back off with the questions, she wasn't going to take it. "Then you might not want this job, Mr. Burke."

"Zack," he reminded her.

"Zack. We don't have a bunkhouse. My older brother lives in the house up the lane, and Marty lives here. You'd have a room in this house with the family."

He pushed back his chair as if to push away from her and the whole idea. "You're kidding!"

Lucy shook her head. "No, I'm not. You'd have a room on this floor down the hall and you'd take your meals with us."

Before the man across from her could respond, the telephone rang. With an "Excuse me, I'll be right back," Lucy stood, went into the living room and picked up the phone.

After another glance at Zack, she answered, "Hello, McIntyres."

"Lucy, is that you? It's John Buckley."

"Mr. Buckley! How are you?"

"I'm fine. Do you have a minute?"

John Buckley was the family lawyer. What could he possibly want with her? "What is it?"

"I'd like you to stop in at my office. I have something I want you to see."

"I don't understand."

"The lawyer who handled your adoption died. Records were sent on to me. There's not much, but there is a picture you should look at."

"What kind of picture?"

"I think you should see it before we decide what, if anything, we want to do about it. I'd email it to you but

I'd like you to see the original. When are you coming into town?"

Long Brush with its quaint shops, professional offices and small hospital was a fifteen-mile trip, and she usually combined shopping and errands when she made it. She could make time on Monday…

She hadn't thought about her origins and her adoption in a long time. All she knew about her birthmother was that the woman had been too poor to keep her and take care of her so she'd given Lucy up for adoption as soon as she was born. That's it. Nothing about her father. No memorabilia. Nothing else. Lucy had been perfectly happy all her life in the McIntyres embrace. Did she want to tamper with that now?

But curiosity was a potent force. "I can be at your office on Monday around one. Will that suit you?"

"I'll be in my office all day. One will be fine. I look forward to seeing you."

After Lucy said good-bye and hung up, she wondered if she should tell her parents about the call. But why upset them? It might be nothing. She'd wait until after her meeting with Mr. Buckley to decide. Right now, she had another decision to make—whether or not she should hire Zackary Burke.

Glad for a chance to regroup, Zack watched Lucy McIntyre walk into the living room and answer the phone. Her warm brown eyes slid over him once more before she looked away and concentrated on her call.

Disconcerted by his body's reaction not only to her gaze but to her mere nearness, he tried to dismiss it as a fluke. For a very long time he'd felt no desire for a woman, the same as he'd felt no inclination to go back to practicing medicine. He knew they were connected. He knew he rode across the western states to escape his thoughts as well as the past. Whenever he stayed in one place too long, all of it came rushing back.

But from the moment he'd taken Lucy McIntyre's hand, smelled lilacs—a scent he associated with long-ago and far-away dreams and white picket fences, and seen the light dusting of freckles across her nose, he'd felt the very real response of a man to a pretty woman. How could he stay when he was attracted to her? How could he stay when he knew any attraction would have no place to go? Not after Kay and what had happened to her and their baby...

Lucy came back to the kitchen, her expression pensive.

"Bad news?" he asked, then wondered why he had. For the past fifteen months he'd tried to stay uninvolved in other people's lives.

"Oh, I wasn't thinking about the call." She smiled. "Actually, I was thinking about you and whether I should hire you."

As she drew closer, the lilacs wound about him again, tempting him with more than a job on a ranch. The freshness of her smile packed the same mighty punch. So he asked gruffly, "Why would you want hired help to stay in your house?"

"That's the kind of people my parents are. But that's also why we checked your references carefully."

"How do you know I'm not an escaped convict?"

"Are you?" she asked with a challenging tilt of her head.

He felt an unexpected laugh rumble from his chest. It had been a long time since he'd really laughed. "Do you honestly think I'd tell you?"

Planting her hands on her hips, she gave him another good once-over with her warm brown eyes. "Yes."

Her certainty drew him out of his seat as much as the scent of her perfume, and he approached her slowly. "Either you're very naive or a very good judge of character."

"Neither, Mr. Burke…Zack," she amended. "I've learned to trust my instincts, and they're telling me my family has nothing to fear from you."

Lucy was slender and tall, but he still towered over her a good five inches. Yet he could tell she wasn't intimidated. "You're right. Your family has nothing to fear from me…if I take the job."

"Do you want it?" Her hands dropped to her sides and he realized he'd like to feel the touch of her skin against his once again.

Impressed with Lucy and her directness, he took a deep breath, knowing he should jump on his Harley and head for far away places right now. But he wanted the work. He needed the satisfaction of physical labor so he could sleep at the end of the day. A ranch would provide plenty of that. "I want the job."

Their gazes held. The awareness between them almost hummed in the kitchen as the full realization that they'd be sleeping under the same roof hit him. Maybe she was thinking about it, too.

Lucy broke eye contact first and took a step back.

"Well, good. I'll give you a brief tour, then show you where to put your things. By then—"

The kitchen door opened and a little boy—about five—came running in. When he saw Zack and Lucy, he stopped. "Are you the man who's gonna help Dad and Gramps and Lucy till Uncle Marty's okay again?"

Zack watched Lucy's chagrin and he guessed this child heard a lot more than the adults wanted him to hear. Zack wondered what the story was with "Marty." Not that it was any of his business.

Lucy said, "This is my nephew, Josh. My oldest brother's son. Josh, this is Mr. Burke and he is going to be working here for a while."

Josh stood in front of Zack and stared up at him. "Is that your bike out there?"

The boy's brown eyes twinkled with curiosity. His reddish hair spiked in more than one direction, while his sweatshirt proclaimed he was a COWBOYS fan. Zack's heart ached for the son he'd lost, the child who'd lost his life before he'd had the chance to begin it. He hadn't been around children since Kay and their baby died. He'd avoided contact just as he'd avoided the feelings that hurt too much to name.

But he guessed he wasn't going to be able to avoid Josh. "Yep. That's my bike."

"Can I have a ride on it?"

"Josh…" Lucy scolded.

Zack grinned. "I bet we'll have to ask a few grown-ups before I can give you an answer on that."

Turning to Lucy, Josh pleaded, "If you ask Dad, I'll ask Mom. Please?"

Zack could tell Lucy was putty in her nephew's hands. He was sure of it when she gave the boy a hug and said, "I'll see what I can do."

"Josh, I told you not to run ahead of me like that." A pleasantly rounded woman, wearing a down coat smiled at Zack from the doorway. As she stepped into the kitchen, Zack realized she belonged here as much as the hand-woven multi-colored place mats on the table, the green vines sitting in planters on the window ledge, and the homey aroma of something braising in the oven.

Coming right up to Zack, she extended her hand. "I'm Esther McIntyre."

The manners he'd thought he'd left back in California but that had emerged with Lucy and now with her mother, urged him to say, "It's good to meet you, Mrs. McIntyre. I've accepted the job on the ranch. That is unless you'd like to interview me, too."

Esther smiled at him, squeezed his hand and looked him straight in the eye. "I trust my husband's judgment and Lucy's, too." Unzipping her coat, she said, "Now, I've got to get supper ready. Lucy, you show Mr. Burke around. And Josh—"

"I wanna go with them."

It didn't look as if Zack had to worry about anything happening even if he was attracted to Lucy. There were lots of chaperones. Maybe this stay at the Rising Star was exactly the distraction he needed. And if it wasn't?

He'd leave. He'd gotten very good at that.

With Josh along on the tour chattering and pointing to his house that was as close to the all-purpose barn as the home where Lucy had grown up, she felt comfortable walking beside Zack. At least that's what she told herself as he responded to Josh's questions and comments with patience and interest.

When the five-year-old ran ahead, she couldn't help but say, "You're good with Josh. Have you spent much time around children?"

Zack stopped for a moment, keeping his gaze trained on the little boy. "Not nearly enough," he answered softly.

Lucy thought she heard longing in his voice and analyzed what it meant. Like most men, he wanted children. Like Pete Cantrell. And when she'd told Pete she couldn't give him a child... He'd practically left a cloud of dust behind him as he'd rushed to escape their relationship. Since Pete, she'd concentrated on her family, the ranch, business management courses, and thought about adopting a child herself someday. She knew better than to repeat past mistakes. She knew better than to expect a man to give up the idea of blood heirs to take care of someone else's children.

She had no reason to believe Zackary Burke was any different. As she gazed at his profile, the defined bone structure, the angular line of a strong jaw, the thick vitality of his black hair, her heart sped up. Yes, she was attracted to him. But attraction was as insubstantial as smoke. There was no point exploring her attraction to him...no future in letting sparks catch fire. Because after the fire, she had nothing to offer.

Zack started walking again and she did, too, keeping her distance, reminding herself he was a drifter and would not be staying.

Glancing at Lucy as she grew quiet, Zack realized she had to take two steps to his one and he slowed his pace. "Tell me about the ranch."

She smiled then, and he realized it was an automatic response to the place where she'd grown up. "When I was little, I thought it was the world," she said. "It seemed to have no boundaries. I could run in any direction until I was too tired to keep going, and I was still on the ranch. I can't imagine living in a big city with no land around me, no cottonwoods or fence or as much grass as sky."

"You love it here."

"I always have, and I always will."

Stopping again, he faced her, suddenly filled with the need not only to get closer to smell her perfume, but to know more about her. "You don't have a desire to venture beyond the town of Long Brush?"

"I'd need a very good reason. Even to live in town. I like being out here with my family."

He itched to touch the glossiness of her hair as it swept across her cheek. "You don't feel crowded? As if they're in your business all the time?" He'd never known real family. He and Kay had been planning to put down roots…

"That's the greatest advantage to living on a ranch. When I feel crowded, I have plenty of space to catch my breath."

Wanting to keep her talking, he asked, "Do you sell your horses locally?"

Lucy raised her chin a notch and stuffed her bare

hands in the pockets of her jacket. "Rising Star has a reputation. We sell to customers all over the country. The Quarter Horse isn't only a cow pony. He's a great all-around horse. And Quarter Horse racing is picking up again, too, though most of the horses we sell are trained for cutting events."

The late October breeze carried the forecast of winter as it suddenly buffeted Zack with more force. When Lucy's hair blew across her lips, he couldn't keep himself from reaching out, smoothing it along her cheek. Her brown hair was as silky as it looked. Would her lips taste as sweet as he imagined? Could her hands make him remember passion and the fire that drove it?

If he lowered his head, he could taste her...maybe taste desire again...

"Hey, Mr. Burke," Josh called from the barn door. "Come see my saddle."

Lucy's lashes fluttered and she avoided his gaze. Zack pushed desire away and said to Josh," "We'll be right there." More disappointed than he wanted to admit that he hadn't kissed her, he was also grateful for the interruption. What if he'd kissed her and found he was still frozen inside? And what if she thought a kiss meant something other than curiosity?

As he saw Lucy's cheeks redden not only from the fresh air, but also from the embarrassment she was trying to hide, he knew a kiss would mean more to a woman like this than a moment of desire.

Then all of a sudden, she faced him squarely and asked, "When you leave Rising Star, where are you headed?"

The question took him by surprise—but only for a moment. He realized Lucy, like most women, had permanence on her mind. He'd learned too well that nothing about life was permanent. "Trying to get rid of me already?" he teased.

"Of course not. I just wondered, that's all."

He could tell Lucy wasn't the type of woman who could be easily sidetracked. "Probably Texas."

"Any place in particular?"

Frowning, he shrugged as if he hadn't given it much thought. "San Antonio, maybe."

"Why?"

"Is this still part of the interview?" he asked, impatient with her questions because he didn't have the answers.

"I guess you can say that. Where a man is going can be just as important as where he's been."

He'd been to hell and was finding his way back to earth. Holding on to anger that simmered beneath his impatience, he answered, "I'm going to San Antonio because I've never been there."

"And after that?" she pressed some more.

Raking his hand through his hair, he said, "I haven't planned it out. Maybe I'll head up to Alaska and climb a few glaciers."

Lucy didn't blink an eye. "What are you running from, Zack?"

Her insight brought his anger to the surface. "I'm not running. I'm exploring. And I didn't realize when I accepted this job that I'd be grilled about my life. Or are you reconsidering your offer?"

"No, the offer holds. If you still want the job."

For some insane reason, he wanted it more now than when he'd ridden his bike under the wooden sign where letters carved into the wood read RISING STAR.

"Mr. Burke. Aunt Lucy. Are you coming?" Josh yelled again, holding the door open for them.

After waving to her nephew, Lucy waited for Zack's answer.

When her brown eyes searched his face, Zack realized this woman might have the power to make him feel again. "Look, I want the job. But I want my privacy, too. Let's just stick to the here and now."

Her brows arched. "A man without a past and without a future. We can try it, Zack. But I can't promise my family won't ask the same questions I have. You might get tired of fending them off."

With a grimace, he shook his head. "Let's go look at Josh's saddle. I'll worry about fending off your family when I have to."

As he strode toward Josh, Zack realized Lucy's words were more of a prediction than a warning. At least he'd be ready.

And he *would* be prepared. He wasn't about to open wounds that were finally starting to heal.

Zack met the McIntyres as they straggled in for Saturday night supper. Josh introduced each member as if it was the most important job he ever had. Zack suspected Esther McIntyre had suggested the procedure to Josh as an exercise in social skills but also to make Zack feel more comfortable. He was definitely a fish out of water in this family atmosphere.

Mary Jo McIntyre, Rick's wife, dressed in jeans and flannel blouse, her light brown hair pulled back in a ponytail, sparkled with the same enthusiasm for life as her son. "It's good to meet you, Mr. Burke. I hope Josh hasn't been too much of a bother."

"No bother at all. He makes a great tour guide."

Mary Jo smiled and ruffled her son's hair. "He knows more about this ranch than I do. He sees and hears everything."

Zack laughed. Twice in one day. How long had it been since laughter had been part of his life?

When Rick McIntyre shook Zack's hand, his grip was firm, his gaze friendly. "Lucy asked me Josh's very important question. How about you and I take a turn around the place on your bike sometime before I give Josh the okay?"

Zack heard the amusement in Rick's suggestion. "No problem. In fact, you might even want to try it by yourself."

Rick grinned like a teenager. "I was hoping you'd say that. I think you and I will get along just fine."

When Tom McIntyre came in, he went to the kitchen, hugged his wife and dropped a kiss on her cheek. Then he joined the group in the living room. With a grip as strong as his oldest son's, he shook Zack's hand. "I understand you roared in here on a motorcycle. Maybe we can convince you a Quarter Horse is a much better means of transportation."

Lucy crossed to her father with a smile. "Better watch it, Zack. He's the best salesman in the state of Wyoming."

Her father grinned at her affectionately. "You know as well as I do our horses sell themselves. I just find them good riders." He looked Zack up and down. "Something tells me, this man is a good rider."

Before Zack could respond, the door flew open and everyone turned toward it. A younger version of Tom McIntyre stood in the doorway, a load of firewood stacked high in his arms.

Tom said in a low voice to Lucy, "We actually got some work out of him today. Maybe he's gonna stop mopin' about that girl."

"Dad…," Lucy chided.

"He's got to get on with his life. You know that better than anyone."

Lucy glanced quickly at Zack, then looked away. But not before he saw the shadows in her eyes, not before he saw her chagrin that he'd overheard her dad's remark. Apparently something…or some*one*…had hurt her.

Marty dumped the logs on the hearth by the fireplace, then turned toward the group gathered around it. Unlike the other McIntyres, he made no move toward Zack.

After a moment of silence where the atmosphere in the room suddenly became awkward, Lucy introduced the two men. "Marty, this is Zack Burke. He'll be working with us for a while."

Marty's dark brown eyes focused on Zack, switched to his sister, then back to Zack. "So you did it. Fine. I didn't know bringing in hired help was an occasion for a party, though. We usually only have this commotion on Sundays."

Esther, standing in the doorway to the living room, addressed her son. "We're a family everyday. I wanted Zack to feel welcome."

"Welcome to the ranch," Marty said automatically, with no real feeling, but because it was expected of him. Then he headed for the stairs and disappeared before he could be chided for his rudeness.

Zack couldn't help but be curious about this member of the McIntyre family who was so different from the others.

Lucy came to stand beside Zack, her arm brushing his. "I'm sorry about his attitude. He's had rough going lately."

Rick frowned. "A lot of that rough going is his own fault. More than once I told him Angie wasn't ready to get serious, but he wouldn't listen. He wouldn't take advice then, just like he won't take advice now. He's as hard-headed as they come."

Mary Jo nudged her husband's arm with a small smile. "As if you know nothing about being hard-headed. Lucy's the only one of the McIntyre siblings who knows how to bend."

"Are you saying I'm stubborn?" Rick asked with mock indignation.

Mary Jo laughed. "That's a pleasant way of putting it."

Tom shook his head. "Stubborn or not, that boy better get his head together. Lucy, try to talk some sense into him again, will you? Of any of us, he listens to you best."

"I'll try, Dad."

When she turned toward her father and her elbow brushed Zack, electric charges danced up his arm.

Esther beckoned to them. "Come on! Supper's ready. When we're sitting around the table, maybe Marty will realize how much he still has."

Josh maneuvered to sit on Zack's left. Lucy sat on his right. When Marty rejoined his family, he positioned himself across from the two of them.

It had been over two years since Zack had sat down and eaten a home-cooked family dinner. The night before his camping trip with Kay…

Rick asked, "So…Zack. What do you do besides ride around on a bike?"

Zack accepted the platter of roast beef Lucy passed to him and considered his options. He didn't want to lie to these people but he also didn't want to answer questions that would lead to areas he'd rather avoid. Noticing Lucy's "I-warned-you" look, he answered, "Along with working on ranches, some construction jobs. I've done a little bit of everything. Mr. McIntyre, I hear that construction is particularly slow in Wyoming. Why do you think that is?"

Fortunately for Zack, the conversation turned to the housing market and the economic conditions in Long Brush and the surrounding area. Then he concentrated on his food and tried to keep his mind off Lucy as she reached for the salt shaker. Her hair swayed along her cheek—silky, soft, natural.

Suddenly, she leaned close to his shoulder. "You managed that one like a pro."

If Zack turned his head, his chin would brush her hair. He tightened his hand into a fist, inhaled her scent, and said as casually as he could manage, "I know a secret. Most people like to talk about what concerns them."

"I'll remember that," she said with a smile in her voice.

He turned his head then and his chin did brush her hair. His chest tightened and all his senses went on red alert until suddenly Josh tugged on Zack's arm. Turning from Lucy, he felt Marty's stabbing gaze on him as he leaned down to the five-year-old.

After supper, Marty followed Zack to the living room.

Zack stood at the fireplace and waited. If Lucy's brother had something to say, he might as well get it off his chest.

It didn't take long until he did. "Lucy hired you mighty quick."

Zack faced Marty squarely. "You don't trust her judgment?"

"I don't trust a stranger who looks at her the way you do. I'm just warning you—we protect our own. So watch your step."

Zack wondered just how he *did* look at Lucy. As if he wanted to touch her, and kiss her, and wrap his body around hers? He thought he was more guarded than that. Yet, there was no point denying his attraction to her, and he wouldn't lie about it. "Lucy and I are adults. What happens between us is our business."

"Lucy is a McIntyre."

"That doesn't mean you can run her life."

"No, but I can watch out for her like I always have."

As Rick and Mary Jo entered the living room, Marty moved away, leaving Zack to realize more fully what it meant to be a member of a family. An ache for the wife and son he'd lost filled him...an ache he'd managed to deny for over two years.

Chapter Two

Long Brush, Wyoming, nestled in a valley at the foot of the Big Horns. Because of the protection of the mountains, the weather wasn't as extreme in this area as in other areas of the state. But this last day of October carried the promise of much colder weather as Lucy walked briskly to John Buckley's office after parking her car at the curb.

Although her mind should be on this meeting with her family's attorney, she couldn't stop thinking about Zack, about the way she felt whenever she saw him or got close to him. He'd made himself scarce yesterday after morning chores and roared off on his motorcycle until evening when he'd helped feed the horses and then disappeared into his room. He'd been wearing a Stetson and an insulated vest last night and she wondered if he'd purchased supplies for his stay. They'd exchanged quick looks at breakfast this morning as her dad had filled him in on the chores for the day. Marty had slept late again and her father intended to see exactly how handy Zack could be on a horse. She'd watched for a while but realized Zack could take command of a horse as well as anything else. She'd stepped up her own work training horses in the arena so she could arrive in Long Brush by one.

Lucy climbed the brick steps to John Buckley's office and turned the large brass knob. As she entered the waiting area, she smelled old wood and lemon polish. The attorney's long-time secretary looked up from her desk. "Hi, Lucy. How's your mom and dad?"

Everyone in Long Brush seemed to know everyone else. It added to Lucy's sense of belonging. "They're good."

"John's waiting for you. Go ahead in."

The door to John Buckley's office stood ajar. Lucy pushed it open and stepped inside.

Lucy had seen Mr. Buckley on occasion. He'd come to the ranch over the years to talk to her father about legal matters. Every Christmas the McIntyres hosted a party and invited friends and business acquaintances. That was the last Lucy had spoken with Mr. Buckley until his phone call.

The older man sat behind his desk, papers spread on his blotter. He stood. "It's nice to see you, Lucy."

"It's good to see you, too. Your call surprised me."

He motioned to the chair in front of his desk. "The envelope that arrived surprised me." When Lucy sat, he did the same and took a manila folder from a basket on his desk.

"You have more information about my birth mother?" Lucy had never asked questions. She hadn't wanted to know anything about the woman who had given her away. All these years she'd only known that when her mom couldn't have more children, she and her dad had brought her home and loved her.

"Not more exactly. I already had a copy of the fact sheet. Your mother has a copy, too. Merely vital statistics. This was a private adoption. Your parents were a little older than some and wanted a little girl to add to their family. Through a contact I found out you were available. We accepted the documents and information we were given. But now, in the package I was sent, I found this." He flipped a photograph onto the desk in front of her.

Lucy picked it up and studied it carefully. It was a picture of two baby girls, wrapped in pink blankets with tiny knit caps. Two *identical* baby girls. She'd paged through her parents' photo albums many times, through countless photographs of her joining the McIntyre family. She remembered how she looked in those youngest photos from babyhood throughout her childhood. One of the infants in this picture was undoubtedly her. But who was the other one?

"What do you think this means?" Her heart pounding, she was almost afraid to put her own guess into words.

"I think you have a sister. From the photo, I'd say a twin sister."

Lucy felt almost dizzy as her world spun and she continued to stare at the Polaroid photograph. The McIntyres had welcomed her into their family and loved her. She called her parents Mom and Dad. She loved them. They loved her. She couldn't have asked for a better childhood. But…

She'd always felt part of her was missing. Over the years, she'd relegated the feeling to the fact that her birth mother, Jeanette Sullivan, had abandoned her. No matter what the reasons, she'd given Lucy away. She hadn't wanted her. Lucy had accepted the feelings that accompanied that knowledge as part of her personality. And through the love of her adopted family, she'd decided that just because her birth mother didn't love her, that didn't mean others couldn't.

Yet now... Maybe a part of her had always been missing. A twin sister! As soon as she thought about it, she squashed her enthusiasm. What if it wasn't so? What if this picture wasn't of her? What if...?

"Lucy, we can pursue this if you'd like. We can try to find out if Jeanette Sullivan bore more than one child. Would you like me to try?"

Jeanette Sullivan. A stranger's name. Her birth mother's name.

Lucy was afraid to hope and lose. It had happened to her in the past. Growing up, she'd thought about the day when she'd be married, have children of her own who would always know they were loved. But when she was seventeen, she'd jumped a fence that was too high. The horse fell on her and after surgery, she'd been informed she'd never be able to have children. So she'd given up that hope.

When she'd met Pete Cantrell, she'd reworked her dreams. She could get married and adopt children, making sure those children always knew they were loved. She could have a good life with Pete. But when she'd told Pete she couldn't have children, he'd reacted as if she were damaged goods. He hadn't called for weeks afterwards, making his feelings clear. She'd given up the hope of marriage, deciding she could herself adopt some day.

Now, she was afraid to hope she had a twin, afraid to look and not find. More dreams shattered? And she didn't only have her life to consider. How would such a search affect her parents? Her brothers? Would they be hurt? Would they think they weren't enough? That all the love they'd given her over the years wasn't sufficient?

"Lucy?" John Buckley was waiting for her answer.

"Mr. Buckley, I have to think about this. You haven't told my parents anything about it, have you?"

"No. The records are yours. The picture belongs to you. You can take it with you if you'd like. I scanned it into the computer."

Lucy straightened a corner of the photo that had gotten bent. Then she slipped it into her purse and stood. "I'll let you know what I decide."

John Buckley stood, too. "I don't know what you're thinking, but the older I get, the more I realize how important family is. Any family. All family."

Crossing to the door, her heart pounding, she responded, "I'll keep that in mind."

As Lucy left the lawyer's office and stood outside in the cold air, she felt like crying and didn't understand why. Her secure life felt shaken in some way. Even if she didn't pursue a search, nothing would ever be quite the same. In her purse she carried a link to the past and maybe a link to the future.

She held her purse against her heart and hurried to her car.

The four-poster pine bed in the only first-floor bed-room was comfortably firm, the patchwork quilt adding just the right amount of weight to the sheet and blanket. But for the third night in a row, Zack couldn't sleep. It seemed like hours since he'd been lying in the bed, staring into the black of the room.

Maybe he should call Linc. Then again, maybe he shouldn't. Linc Granger had been married less than a year and he still sounded like a newlywed whenever Zack spoke with him. His friend was a lucky man. Zack was happy for him and grateful for everything Linc had done since Zack had left L.A. In fact, he should be hearing from his friend soon. With Zack's power of at-torney, Linc would be handling the settlement on the condo soon.

Zack pushed his pillow into a different position. Why couldn't he let the fatigue from riding and work-ing outdoors overtake him?

Because sights and sounds of the McIntyres kept running through his head. Especially Lucy. She'd looked pale at supper tonight. Bothered by something. And she'd gone to her room after she'd helped clean up, saying she had assignments to finish for her online col-lege course. He wondered if she regretted hiring him. Because whenever their eyes met…

The night silence was abruptly broken by a loud clatter. Zack sat up and listened closely. Footsteps from the living room to the kitchen. From the kitchen to the living room.

He might as well explore because he obviously wasn't going to sleep. Grabbing his jeans, he quickly slid them on.

As he approached the living room, he caught the flash of a pink robe at the corner of the sofa. Closer, he could see Lucy patting the padded arm with a towel. A mug sat on the second tier of the table beside the light.

"Need help?" he asked softly.

Her hand went to her breast and, even though he'd spoken quietly, he could see he'd startled her. In pink chenille Lucy was every bit as tempting, if not more so, than Lucy dressed in casual clothes. Her robe was long, flowing to her ankles, but her feet were bare. A white nightgown patterned with small rosebuds showed in the V of her robe, the ruffled cuffs peeking out from the wide sleeves.

She looked cuddly and soft and…the way that she was staring at him made his blood run faster. He hadn't bothered with a shirt, and he'd left the button on his jeans unfastened. Her gaze passed over his chest to the dip at his waist.

Her cheeks grew rosy and she cleared her throat. "I thought everyone was asleep."

The temptation to kiss Lucy became a pressing urge. His voice was husky when he said, "So did I."

She folded the towel and laid it on the coffee table. "I was having a cup of tea and got distracted. I spilled it."

Moving closer, he sensed more was going on for her than insomnia. "What's wrong, Lucy?"

Her gaze flicked to something on the coffee table, a Polaroid photo. "I have a decision to make."

He leaned across the table and picked up the picture. Two babies. Two baby girls. The photograph was obviously old, but he didn't understand its connection to Lucy. "Who are they?"

"One of them is me."

The turmoil in her eyes drew him to her as much as everything else about her. From the first moment he'd met Lucy, she'd been poised and confident. The woman standing before him now looked more like a lost little girl.

Holding the photo, he stepped around the other side of the table and sank down on the couch. "You have a sister?"

Lucy sat in the corner of the sofa and pulled one leg up under her as she turned toward him. "I'm adopted, Zack."

That was the last thing he expected. "You're not serious!" Realizing his response might have insulted her, he said, "I'm sorry. It's just that you have such a close family. Your relationship with your parents—" He stopped.

"Mom and Dad adopted me a few days after I was born and have never for a moment made me feel 'adopted.' And Rick and Marty…they've always been my brothers."

Zack laid the picture in her lap. "So how does this fit in?"

"The lawyer who handled the adoption for my birth-mother died. Paperwork was sent to the attorney here who handled the adoption for my parents. This picture was in the packet."

"And what decision do you have to make?"

"Mr. Buckley contacted me about the picture. He suspects I have a twin sister somewhere and wants to know if he should start a search to find her."

"You haven't told him to go ahead?"

She shook her head.

"Why?"

"I don't want to hurt my family."

"Why would finding your sister hurt your family?"

Lucy stared at the photo with longing. When she looked up, her eyes glistened. "This family has given me more love than I could ever need. They've protected me and supported me and loved me unconditionally through everything. How can I tell them I want to undertake a search for a woman I don't know? Why should I search for more when I already have so much?"

"Isn't life about searching for more?"

"Is that what you're doing?" she asked softly.

He shook his head. "This isn't about me. It's about you. You can't let gratitude stand in the way of what you need to do for yourself."

"It's not just gratitude. I don't want my family to think they're not enough."

"That's a cover, Lucy. What are you afraid of?"

Her eyes changed to the darkest brown as she dropped her legs over the edge of the sofa. "You don't know what you're talking about."

As she stood, he clasped her wrist. "I know having a connection somewhere in this world and not being able to reach it hurts like hell. So before you make a final decision about searching or not searching, figure out what it means for the rest of your life."

She gazed into his eyes for a long silent moment. Then she gave a slight tug and he let her pull away.

"I shouldn't have confided in you," she murmured.

"Because you don't like my advice or because you're afraid I'll spill the beans?"

"Because this kind of decision is one that has to feel right in my heart. No amount of advice will affect that."

As she tucked the photograph in her pocket and started for the stairs, Zack called, "Lucy?"

She paused.

"I *will* keep your secret. I don't take confidences lightly."

"Thank you, Zack."

He gave a slight shrug. "No big deal. Good night."

His gaze followed her as she climbed the stairs, and he knew Lucy confiding in him was a big deal. It was a privilege...and a bond that could only cause pain because he'd have to sever it.

He couldn't stay. He couldn't get closer to Lucy because he never wanted to feel the pain of loss again.

The horse's wild eyes and prancing didn't scare Lucy as she stood very still, letting the animal get used to her presence. She'd gentled horses like this before...horses that had been mishandled out of cruelty or ignorance. One of their neighbors kept his eyes open when he went to auctions because he knew Lucy was good at helping an animal like this.

She stayed outside the stall at the corner opposite the feed box, softly crooning to the chestnut gelding. "You're going to like it here. I promise you will. No one's going to hurt you. Why don't you try some of those oats? You have to eat to get healthy again."

"He'd probably like a cube of sugar more."

The deep masculine voice startled Lucy and her new horse. The chestnut side-stepped.

"Whoa, boy, it's okay," Lucy soothed. "He won't hurt you, either."

The horse, somewhat used to Lucy's voice because she'd been talking to him for the past half hour, stared warily at Zack. When Zack approached, the gelding reared up.

"Whoa," Lucy said in an authoritative but calming tone. "Whoa, boy. Easy. Zack, back up a little, will you? I think he has more of a problem with men than women. Rick had a rough time getting him off the trailer."

As Zack stepped back a few feet, Lucy climbed to the second rung of the stall and crooned until the horse quieted. "Good boy," she encouraged. Taking a carrot out of her back jeans pocket, she broke it in half and dropped it into the feed trough.

Then she climbed down slowly and crossed to Zack. He was standing by bales of hay, watching her with an intensity that always unnerved her. She didn't know why she had confided in him last night. Maybe because she couldn't stop thinking about the photo and the sister she might have. When he'd questioned her, some of those thoughts had spilled out. The point was—they wouldn't have just spilled out to anyone.

Tossing and turning a few hours after their talk, she'd decided her best bet was to keep her distance from Zack. She'd eaten breakfast after her dad and Zack had ridden off, and she'd worked with the horses till late in the afternoon. Until this horse had arrived.

"I saw Rick in the corral. He told me about the horse. What are you going to do with him?" Zack asked, keeping his voice low.

In his jeans, boots and flannel shirt, Zack looked at home in the barn. "Comfort him. Prove to him not all human beings are alike."

"And what will you do with him afterward?"

"That depends on his disposition. But usually I can find a kind family and a good home."

"You've done this before."

"Once or twice a year, depending how much patience and care each horse takes."

"Your dad said you'll give the horse away. Certainly you could get something for your time and expenses."

"I don't do this for money, Zack. I do it…just to give back."

"Give back?" He asked with an arched brow.

"Yes. For the life I've had that could have been much different."

"There's that gratitude again," Zack muttered.

He sounded as if he resented it and she wondered why. "What's wrong with gratitude?"

"I just think it's illogical to give credit to some Power for the good things that happen and then have to take the blame ourselves for the bad stuff."

"I never look at it that way." She hadn't blamed

God for her accident, or herself, either, for that matter. It was just something that had happened. "You know, usually we can take the bad stuff and make something good out of it." Maybe she couldn't have children, but she could give some child a loving home.

Zack's jaw tensed and his shoulders grew rigid as he said, "Sometimes bad is simply bad, can never be fixed, can never bring any good. I think you've been isolated on this ranch for too long."

"I'm not isolated here, Zack, and I don't wear blinders. But I do know what kind of attitude will help me and what kind will hurt me."

"Facing reality never hurt anyone," he insisted with a vehemence she hadn't heard from him before.

"Maybe. But living without faith in something can hurt. What happened to take your faith away?"

After his warning about wanting his privacy, she thought he was going to turn away and walk out. But instead he countered with, "What makes you think I ever had any faith?"

"Instinct," she summed up quickly.

Anger altered his expression until his jaw was as hard as his eyes. "Your *instincts* might be wrong. Maybe you can coax that horse into trusting someone or something again, but you can forget it where I'm concerned." With that, he did turn away and headed for the door.

Lucy sensed that something made Zack restless, urging him to keep moving, to avoid what he didn't want to face. She couldn't be around him without wanting to help. But should she?

Instincts told her the risk to her heart would be far greater than any she'd ever faced.

Her instincts were rarely wrong.

The following evening, Zack made his way to the main barn. Mrs. McIntyre had told him Lucy would either be with the new horse or in her "workroom." Lucy's mother hadn't explained what type of workroom it was. He remembered a closed door next to the tack room, and he'd guessed it led to a storage area. Wherever Lucy was, he'd find her. She'd been different around him since he'd snapped at her yesterday. Too polite. And he didn't like it. He owed her an apology and wasn't quite sure how to go about giving it to her. Maybe when he was alone with her, he'd know.

Lucy stirred up emotions he thought were dead and buried along with his wife and child. Not only did she stir up old emotions, but she instigated new ones. Yet he knew he had nothing to offer her. He was a physician who had rejected practicing medicine, a man who was too restless to stay in one place very long. End of story.

As he went inside the barn, he remembered how noise had startled the gelding the day before. When he spotted Lucy with the horse, he approached her quietly, the scent of hay and wood and leather strong but oddly appealing, somehow comforting in the shadowy barn.

The yellow overhead light shone on her hair, transforming strands to red. He hadn't expected to find her *inside* the stall. But there she was. How else could she gentle an animal who was afraid?

He didn't want to disturb her. The picture of her stroking the horse's neck, the sound of her soft murmurs, tightened Zack's throat and he didn't even know why. Her hand slowly moved from the horse's neck to his flank, the strokes firm and long. Zack imagined exactly how comforting her hands could be. He automatically thought of those strokes in another context…in a bed…with him.

The low tone of her voice was as mesmerizing as the motion of her hand as she said, "Thank goodness we know a lady vet. I told you she wouldn't hurt you."

When Zack took another step toward the stall, Lucy looked up. So did the horse.

Giving the chestnut a few soft pats, she took a piece of carrot out of her back pocket and held it in her palm. The animal shied away, then as Lucy stood perfectly still, he sniffed at her fingers. Finally, he took the carrot, then backed up.

She opened the gate of the box stall and stepped into the walkway.

"It looks as if you're making progress." Zack kept his voice low.

She glanced over her shoulder into the stall. "A little at a time."

"You have a magic touch," he said, partly teasing, partly not. When she didn't respond, he jumped into the silence. "Lucy, I'm sorry about what I said yesterday…about the way I said it."

She looked surprised. "We all have days when there's more dark than light."

What Lucy didn't understand was that all his days were the same. But he didn't want to get into another argument, and he knew they could because their attitudes were so different. At least she'd seemed to accept his apology.

To change the subject, he said, "Your mother told me you had a workroom out here."

She pointed to the far end of the barn. "Over there. Come on. I'll show you."

He followed her down the walkway until they came to the rear of the stable and two doors. The one on the left led to the tack room. Opening the door on the right, she said, "This is supposed to be a place to bunk when we need to spend the night out here. But it's also been my workroom since I had braids."

When he stepped inside, he noticed the bunk beds against the wall. But what caught his attention was the table, the assortment of tools, the wood shavings, and finally the shelves behind the swivel chair that held carved animals of every shape and size. He was drawn to them because he knew they belonged to Lucy and the work of her hands.

The first one he picked up wasn't one of the many horses, but a deer. It was part of a set—a doe, a stately buck and a fawn. He passed his thumb over the wood. "You're very talented."

She laughed. "More determination and preoccupation than talent. I didn't become serious about it until after my... Until I was in my late teens. It's my escape. I come in here some nights when I can't sleep."

Zack set the deer on the shelf and picked up a dog. "Do you sell these?"

She shook her head. "Mostly I make them for Christmas presents. My family teases me about knowing what to expect each year."

"They don't come in here?"

"Rarely. If I'm working on something special, I cover it."

Zack saw the piece of soft flannel draped over one end of the top shelf. He nodded to it. "Do you mind?"

"Go ahead," she said softly.

The carving was the largest on the shelves, about ten inches long and six inches high. When Zack pulled the cloth away, he found a reclining horse and foal.

"That's for my dad."

Zack imagined the hours and hours of work and concentration that had gone into the carving. Somehow, that told him more than anything else exactly how much Lucy loved her father—her whole family. Because he'd bet his boots she'd crafted a gift for every member with the same loving care.

Suddenly he turned toward her. "And what do you want for Christmas, Lucy?"

The golden sparks in her eyes told him something came to her mind immediately and it might have something to do with him. But then she said, "I have everything I need."

He didn't know many people who were content, who weren't always looking for "more." "If St. Nick dropped by this year, what would you *want*?" he pressed.

There was such a sadness in her eyes for a moment. But then it was gone in a flicker as she gave a little shrug. "My wishes aren't tangible. I'd like an easy winter for Mom and Dad. Some happiness for Marty..."

"You, Lucy," Zack interrupted. "What do you want?"

She flushed. "Nothing out of the ordinary."

Her hesitancy, the distance she was trying to keep, should have made him back off. But an inner urge to know drove him to push. "Don't you have dreams?" His gaze wouldn't let hers escape. This woman fascinated him the way no woman ever had. She called out to a deep corner in his soul that was looking for answers.

He saw the change on her face—the moment uncertainty became the confidence he usually found in her. She tilted her head. "And if I asked you about your Christmas dreams, would you tell me what they were?"

Oh ho. So she wasn't as trusting and as open as he might think. "Tit for tat?"

She raised her chin with a bit of temper. "I don't know nearly as much about you as you know about me."

Silence stretched in the small room. "No, you don't." After another long moment, he added, "I don't have Christmas dreams or any others for that matter. I don't dream any more, Lucy. Not since I lost my wife and child."

Chapter Three

Lucy's shock at his statement showed in her widened eyes, the slight opening of her mouth. "How, Zack?"

He was as shocked as she was that it had popped out. Now that it had, he didn't expect her to question him. Yet, knowing Lucy, he should have realized she wouldn't just let it stand, either. For a moment he thought about not answering, walking away, trying to forget—not remember.

But her brown eyes were too deep, the crease in her brow too concerned…about *him*.

"We went camping. To get away. To concentrate on each other. I wasn't sure we should. Kay was seven months pregnant. We were in the middle of nowhere. In the early morning something went terribly wrong. She started having contractions, then hemorrhaging. I rushed her to the nearest hospital. But we were too late and I lost them both."

"Zack, I'm so sorry."

The comfort and compassion in Lucy's eyes made him feel worse instead of better. Why should her caring hurt him, make the pain more real than it had ever been? He tried to pack it back up, put a lid on it as he had for so long. "It's been more than two years. It's over and done."

Lucy touched his arm. "How can a loss like that ever be over and done?"

Pulling away from her, he shook his head. "I can't think about it, Lucy. I had to move on."

"To what, Zack?" she asked, as if he was supposed to know the answer.

The gentle question almost made him angry, but he couldn't be angry with her for asking something he'd avoided for two years. "I don't know yet. I just know I have to leave the past behind. And I don't want to dredge it up. I just told you because…"

"Because I pried."

Torn between wanting to be honest, wanting to give in to his desire for her, wanting to escape the sense of loss he felt as if he'd carried it forever, he finally said, "No. Because I want you to understand we've led very different lives."

Her voice was soft and persuasive in the dusky atmosphere of the barn. "You can still hope and dream."

He closed his eyes for a moment, whether to block out Lucy or the idea, he didn't know. But then he opened them again and saw her waiting…waiting for him to agree with her. And he couldn't. "That's the difference between us, Lucy. You believe in the possibilities. I believe in reality. And reality is telling me I should just keep moving, to grab what I can while I can."

"You're not that kind of man, Zack."

If he stayed in this small room with her any longer, he'd kiss her. Maybe even begin to dream. But kisses and dreams would only lead to disappointment for them both. "You've only known me for two days."

"I think I know what matters."

Her certainty and her compassion, mixed with the desire he already felt, had him reaching out to touch her face. "Lucy McIntyre, you haven't seen enough of the world or enough of men to make any comparisons."

Golden sparks flashed in her eyes. "And what makes you think you know me any better than I know you?"

He had to smile, then. "Touché."

So attuned was he to Lucy's reactions to him, he felt more than saw her shiver. "You're cold. We'd better get back to the house."

She looked as if she wanted to prolong their conversation, but they really had nothing to talk about. She had roots, and family, and stability. Even though she was adopted, she always had. He had no roots anymore. He had no stability anymore. And he'd be moving on. Nope, there was nothing else to say.

Zack waited while Lucy switched off the lights. As they walked back to the house, he said, "You do beautiful work, Lucy. Anyone who receives one of your carvings for Christmas will receive a treasure."

Lucy murmured thank-you, wanting to say a lot more. She wanted to say, *If you stay till Christmas, I can give you one.* But she knew she couldn't persuade Zack to stay if he was determined to go.

When she opened the door into the kitchen, only the light over the sink glowed. "Mom and Dad must have gone up to bed."

"We'd better turn in, too," Zack said as he came into the room.

Lucy thought again about what Zack had told her. The pain in his eyes probably didn't even come close to the pain in his heart. She ached for him. She could hardly imagine his pain…his loss. The problem was he obviously wanted to bury both. That might be a temporary fix, but in the long run burying the grief would only hurt him.

"We could turn in, or we could raid the refrigerator," she offered, hoping she could persuade him to open up a bit more. "There's still some apple pie."

"That's a temptation almost too good to pass up," he responded, his blue eyes telling her he might be tempted by more than the pie.

She wished she'd had more experience with men. She wished… It didn't matter what she wished. "Hot chocolate to go with it or milk?"

He smiled. "Are you making the chocolate?"

She laughed. "If you dish out the pie."

Lucy heated the milk and stirred in the cocoa while Zack took two dishes from the cupboard and slid the slices of pie onto the plates. As he took forks from the drawer, she realized he was becoming familiar with his surroundings. He'd seemed at home tonight at supper with her family, even with Marty at the table, though her brother had left after dessert and hadn't returned home. She could guess where he was but hoped she was wrong.

"You're the first person in a long while who's played checkers with Dad." When she'd left the house after supper, Zack and her dad had started the board game.

"He didn't look too pleased when I beat him."

"*No one* beats Dad," she said with another smile. She could just imagine her dad's expression when Zack won.

"Your father told me he wants me to teach him how to play chess."

"You know how?"

"Sure do."

Wanting to ask questions like—*Where did you learn? Who played with you? What did you do before you started traveling the country?*—she instead reined in her curiosity so Zack could tell her willingly when he was ready. "Dad's wanted to learn for years. He has a set upstairs an old friend of his sent him." She poured the hot chocolate into two mugs, sat the pan in the sink filling it with warm water. When she turned away from the sink, she bumped into Zack.

So naturally, he clasped her by the elbows to steady her. Then his hold had nothing to do with steadying. As she gazed into his eyes, she felt light-headed, tingly, expectant. He pulled her closer.

"Lucy," he groaned, almost as if he wanted her to answer him, to stop him, to keep them both from giving in to the vibrations that had hummed between them since his gaze had met hers through the window.

There was no way in heaven that she wanted to stop him. Desire and excitement and curiosity pushed her to answer him in the only way she could. She leaned even closer, anticipating what could happen next, catching the scent of his skin, her eyes memorizing his beard shadow, her hands longing to touch him in ways she'd never touched a man.

She was still a virgin. And at this moment she was glad because she wanted every sensual "first" she could think of to happen with Zack.

His mouth came down on hers. A wild yearning she'd never experienced urged her to slide her hands up his chest. She felt him shudder.

Sliding his hands into her hair, he demanded more than lips on lips. His tongue pushed into her mouth with a vehemence that took her breath away. Pent-up attraction and emotions and confusion about what Zack could mean to her, how he could hurt her, where he could take her, burst into desire that was fiery and hungry and dangerous. Her heart thudded while her pulse raced. His taste and texture and furious need swept her away.

Until the kitchen door opened.

Until she heard boots on linoleum.

Until Marty fell over a kitchen chair and swore.

Quickly, she pulled away from Zack, not daring to look into his eyes to see what that kiss had meant to him. It had turned her world upside down and she felt as wobbly as Marty looked.

Her brother swayed and bent over, dropping his hands to his knees. Quickly, Lucy crossed to him, curving her arm around him. "I hope you didn't drive home," she scolded.

"Jerry brought me home," he mumbled.

"You have to stop this, Marty. Drinking yourself fuzzy isn't going to solve anything."

"I forget about Angie after a few."

"You forget about everything. And not only when you're drinking."

"Jus' help me to bed," he mumbled.

As Lucy glanced at Zack, she saw he was taking it all in, not looking a bit bothered by the kiss that had rocked her world.

"Need a hand?" he asked her calmly, as if the kiss had never happened.

"No. We'll be fine."

After a last look at Zack that didn't tell her any more than she knew before, Lucy concentrated on maneuvering Marty across the living room and up the stairs, warning herself not to think about Zack's kiss...or its repercussions.

Late Saturday afternoon, Zack's horse trotted along the fence line. He was sure it wouldn't be long before a Wyoming winter set in.

When he'd gotten back to the house right before dusk and asked Lucy's whereabouts, Mrs. McIntyre had told him her daughter had gone for a ride. Giving Zack a few hints as to where Lucy might be, her mother had confided that Lucy often forgot about time when she was riding. If she'd had a day like his, she was probably still thinking about that kiss the other night and what might have happened if Marty hadn't stumbled in.

There'd been strain between them since then—a strain her family was bound to notice.

Not wanting supper to be awkward, he figured they'd better talk about it. And it wasn't only the kiss he wanted to discuss. He wanted to know exactly what was going on with Marty.

Zack found Lucy with her horse tethered to a post. She was standing at the fence, looking across the pasture at the grazing cattle. But he had the feeling she wasn't really seeing anything in her line of vision.

So absorbed in her thoughts, she didn't hear him dismount and didn't notice when he slipped his horse's reins around another post. "Lucy?"

When he approached her, her gaze met his and he could see she remembered everything about their kiss. The telltale signs were in the golden flecks in her eyes, the way she looked at him, then glanced away.

Better not to beat around the proverbial bush. "That kiss never should have happened. I don't want you to think I'm going to take advantage of living under the same roof."

She stayed turned away. "What if I don't feel you took advantage?"

"Then I think we could both be in trouble. It happened because you feel sorry for me and your kind-heartedness—"

Spinning around to face him, she was definitely annoyed at his assessment of her motives. "Get real,

Zack. I don't kiss a man because I feel sorry for him, and I hope that's not the reason you kiss a woman."

Without asking the exact question, he realized she wanted an exact answer. This conversation wasn't about him kissing any woman. Lucy wanted to know why he'd kissed her. He was going to give it to her straight so they both knew where they stood. "I kiss a woman because I want to satisfy a basic need. End of story."

Her pretty brows arched. "And have you kissed a woman since your wife died?" He found her perception irritating at this particular moment. "It doesn't really matter, does it? A kiss is a means to an end. And since I'm going to be leaving in a few weeks, there can be no good end."

The expansive Wyoming silence surrounded them until Lucy started for her horse. "Put that way, I suppose you're right." Reaching for her horse's reins, she dismissed him and the conversation.

He should let her go. He should take the chill in her voice as a sign she understood what he'd said and agreed. But that chill irritated him almost more than her perception. "Does Marty often come home like that?"

She stopped before she could mount. "I told you he's going through a rough patch."

"Do you always hide his condition from your parents?" In his practice, Zack had seen relatives cover for brothers or sisters or mothers or fathers who turned toward a bottle rather than their family or friends.

"I helped him upstairs to bed. That's all," she responded, but her fingers moved back and forth over her horse's reins.

"You're not helping him if you're hiding his problem."

Wearing a frown that was meant either for him or Marty, she insisted, "There's no 'problem', Zack. And even if there was, I don't know why you care. Like you said, you'll be leaving in a few weeks."

After that pointed observation, she climbed on her horse, gave him a quick nudge with her boots and rode back toward the house.

Her final words echoed in the cold air. Why did they sound different when she said them than when he thought them?

Sunday evening dinner at the McIntyres was an event. As always, Lucy had helped her mother bake pies all afternoon and enjoyed doing it. But this Sunday she'd also had an ulterior motive for baking with her mom. She wanted to stay out of Zack's way. She'd ridden away from him yesterday, more hurt than angry, though she'd had no right to feel hurt. Zack had been honest with her. He'd told her why he'd kissed her. There was no reason why she couldn't accept the fact that mere chemistry was at work and leave it at that.

At least that's what her logic told her. She had a much tougher time convincing her heart. At supper last night, she'd made polite conversation, then gone to her room while Zack had taught her father chess. With Mary Jo, Rick and Josh around tonight, she'd managed not to speak to Zack directly. But now, after washing and drying the last of the pots that wouldn't fit into the dishwasher, she knew she'd have to face some casual time with him. Lucy hung the dish towel over the handle of the stove. When she crossed to the archway of the living room, she stopped, surprised by the sight of Josh curled next to Mary Jo, his head against her arm. That was unusual. Her nephew was always in motion. However at this moment, he sat perfectly still.

Zack was seated on the sofa, too, on Josh's other side, explaining the rudiments of the chess pieces to Rick who'd pulled his chair close to the coffee table where the chess board sat. Marty had gone out—to check on the stock, he'd said—but Lucy suspected he just didn't want to engage in conversation.

Lucy glanced at Zack again. Every time they were in the same room together, he was like a powerful magnet, drawing her, fascinating her, exciting her. She knew she should keep her distance because he wanted to keep his.

But every time their eyes met…

"Mommy, I don't feel so good."

Mary Jo immediately sat forward and turned toward her son. "What's wrong, honey?" She put her hand to his forehead. "You do feel warm. I'm going to get Gram's ear thermometer."

Rick said, "If he's sick, we should get him home."

From across the room, Esther asked, "Would you like to lie down?"

Her grandson shook his head.

Zack slid back on the sofa and casually dropped his arm around Josh's shoulders, leaning close to the boy. She heard him ask in a low voice, "What hurts?"

Josh looked up at him. "My throat."

Zack shifted his hand to the back of Josh's neck.

As she watched, Zack's fingers explored the nape of her nephew's neck, then slipped to under his chin. He seemed to know exactly what he was doing.

His thumb pressed under Josh's ear. "Does that hurt?"

The five-year-old nodded.

Returning with the thermometer, Mary Jo pressed it to her son's ear, then removed it. "Less than a hundred," she said after examining it.

Zack ruffled Josh's hair. "Probably a virus."

With a determined expression, Esther rose from her chair by the fireplace. "I have chicken soup in the freezer. You can take some along."

"I'll get our coats," Rick said, then added, "Better yet, I'll go get the truck and pick Josh up."

Tom McIntyre winked at his grandson. "Seems to me I have a new coloring book in the closet. Would you like to take it along?"

Josh nodded.

Mary Jo went to the kitchen with her husband. As Lucy crossed to Josh, Zack said, "Come over here by the light, partner. I want to see if your throat's red."

As Zack moved with Josh toward the end table light, he explained mildly. "I thought I'd check his throat."

She watched as Josh opened his mouth for Zack and couldn't help asking, "Do you know what you're looking for?"

Zack shrugged. "I've had a few sore throats in my life."

He motioned to Lucy to come look at her nephew's throat. "See the white spots?" he asked.

She looked more carefully, then nodded.

"That means it's a virus."

"Mary Jo will probably call the doctor tomorrow. She doesn't take any chances."

Zack nodded. "If only I'd had a second chance..." he murmured as if thinking out loud.

He didn't have to finish. Lucy could see the anguish in his eyes and hear the loss. "Maybe you will someday."

For a moment, emotion blazed in Zack's eyes, the desire to find the happiness he'd lost. And for that moment Lucy believed it could include her. Then she remembered. She couldn't conceive or bear children. But more importantly, Zack was still running from his future, not embracing it.

Lucy's father returned to the living room with the coloring book he'd promised his grandson. He handed it to Josh. "You stay quiet and listen to your mom until you feel better."

"Can't I come over after school tomorrow?"

Lucy crouched down beside her nephew. "You probably won't be going to school tomorrow. But I'll come visit you and see how you're doing."

After Mary Jo brought Josh his jacket, she waited until he zipped it. Then she hugged and kissed Lucy, hugged her father-in-law, and smiled good-bye to Zack.

Lucy studied the expression on Zack's face as he watched them leave. The longing in it almost broke her heart. "Zack?"

"Do you know how lucky you are?" His voice was gruff.

Nodding, she responded, "Yes, I do. That's why I'm afraid to believe I deserve any more."

Glancing at her father who was stirring the fire, she remembered the picture in her dresser drawer. A few times each day, she studied that photo, staring at herself and the image of the baby who might be her sister. But she was afraid to tempt fate…afraid to upset the family balance.

Zack said in a low voice, "Everyone deserves all the happiness they can find. But you need the courage to take a few risks."

"Is that advice for me or yourself?"

"Lucy," he said with an exasperated edge.

"Risks aren't so simple, Zack."

He looked deep into her eyes, making her heart race. Then he agreed, "You're right. They're not. It's easy to give advice. Much harder to take it. Maybe we both ought to make a New Year's resolution to keep our advice to ourselves."

Why did his pulling back, his insistence not to get involved hurt her so much? He was a stranger—a man who would move on. She shouldn't care a whit what he thought or felt. But she did. And right now, staying in the same room with him was too uncomfortable for words.

"Dad, I'm going to the barn for a while. I'll see you in the morning."

"Good night, honey. Don't stay out there too late."

She smiled at her father. "I won't." With as neutral

an expression as she could manage, she said, "Good night, Zack."

She thought he said goodnight in return, but she couldn't be sure because she was already in the kitchen.

When Lucy came in from the arena Monday at lunch time, her mother was taking a dust cloth over the furniture.

"Dad and everyone still at the north range?" she asked as casually as she could.

"They're checking the protein blocks. Zack included," her mother added with a sly smile.

Opening the closet door, Lucy hung her short wool, western-patterned jacket on a hanger and didn't respond.

"You like this Zackary Burke, don't you?"

"Mom…"

"It's all right, Lucy, if a man interests you. Not all men are as callous and shallow as Pete Cantrell."

Lucy went to the sink and washed her hands. Pete Cantrell wasn't callous and shallow. He merely wanted a woman who could bear him children. She couldn't. Her mistake had been thinking it didn't matter…thinking that Pete had loved her for who she was, not her child-bearing capabilities. But the failure of their relationship had made her overly cautious about dating or getting involved again.

She really didn't want to explore old history with her mother or think too much about the feelings Zackary Burke had stirred up.

"I have eyes and ears, child. There's something afoot between you and Zack."

"There's nothing going on."

"Lucy, honey, there's tons going on. Most of it under the surface. Why don't you let it rise up?"

"He lost his wife and child, Mom. He's trying to escape his grief. He can't wait to get back on the road. Besides that…" She didn't have to finish it because her mother knew what she was going to say.

"A man can love you for yourself, Lucy. Why can't you believe that?"

"Because even though Zack's still in pain over the loss of his child, he's wishing he could have his chance back. He'll want children again. He's that kind of man." Talking about this with her mother wouldn't change anything.

"You haven't told him you can't have children?"

"That's a subject that's too personal to bring up out of nowhere."

"He told you about his wife and child," her mom said with a lift of her brows.

"Yes, he did, but…"

Esther crossed to her daughter and took her chin in her hand. "I understand your embarrassment. I understand that you feel something is wrong with you. You need the right person to set you straight. Maybe Zack is that person, maybe he's not. But hiding the facts doesn't make them go away."

"I know that, Mom. But Zack and I just aren't that close for me to confide something so personal."

Her mother gave her a huge hug. "Okay, honey.

You have to live your life the way you see fit. Just remember when there's sparks and smoke, fire isn't far behind. And sometimes fire can liven up your life."

Lucy leaned back. "Or burn the house down."

Esther shook her head. "Sometimes you're as stubborn as Marty. Though he did seem in better spirits this morning. Maybe he's finally feeling better. At least he's not out in the old cabin brooding." Out on the west ridge stood an old cabin Lucy went to when she needed to think. Marty had been riding out there a lot lately.

"Have you eaten lunch yet?" Lucy asked, as much to change the subject as anything else.

"Nope. I was waitin' for you. What are you up to this afternoon?"

"I think I'll go up to Rick's and check on Josh, then work on the computer for a while."

"Maybe you're avoidin' Zack."

"Mom!" Lucy warned again.

"Okay. Okay. It's just, I know you. And before Zack came, you would have ridden out and helped your dad and brothers instead of finding things to do here."

"I need a little distance from Zack right now. I know you mean well, but please don't get the idea of playing matchmaker. You'll just embarrass both of us." Lucy saw the flicker of hurt in her mother's eyes. She hated seeing it there and to make it disappear, she said, "I love you, Mom."

Her mother smiled and the hurt disappeared. "I know you do. And I'll try to stay out of your business. But being in it is a habit, Lucy. That's what family is all about."

Lucy thought again about the photo in her dresser and the hurt she might see in her mother's eyes if she told her about it…if she told her she wanted to search for her "real" sister.

Before she decided to do it, she had to be very sure a search and the results of it were exactly what she wanted.

Chapter Four

Sitting cross-legged on the floor of Mary Jo's living room, helping Josh construct a space station from colorful building blocks, Lucy couldn't seem to keep her mind on what she was doing. When the doorbell rang and Mary Jo opened the door, suddenly Zack was standing there asking how Josh was feeling. This tall cowboy was the exact reason she couldn't concentrate.

He handed Mary Jo a basket of apples. "Esther asked me to bring these over. She said she has more than enough and you might need them."

Josh waved at Zack and said, "I'm stuffy. I keep sneezing."

Zack chuckled. "I'd say your cold is running it's course."

Mary Jo smiled. "I called the doctor and he said to give him the same decongestant we used last time. If he's not better in a day or two, I'm supposed to take him in. I have to check on dinner. Make yourself comfortable."

Zack crossed to Lucy and Josh. "What are you building?"

"A space station! I wanna go to Mars when I'm big."

With a smile, Zack asked, "You don't want to be a rancher like your dad?"

"That, too. I can do both."

"What about you, Lucy?"

Zack's voice rolled over her, making her fingers tremble as she held a blue block in her hand. "What about me?"

"You said you were taking a college course. Do you want to live somewhere besides the ranch?"

"I love the ranch."

"That's not what I asked."

"I'm taking the course so I can help Dad run the Rising Star more efficiently. I like my work here. I could study equine science someplace, but long ago I decided I could learn what I needed from Dad and Rick."

"Your father told me you're the best horse trainer in these parts, and I've seen some of that first-hand. That's a talent that's hard to teach."

She could feel the heat rising to her cheeks. "Dad likes to brag."

"I've watched you. I've never seen anyone handle a horse with more patience or skill."

"Lucy taught Alfredo," Josh said with pride.

"He's the one with the star on his nose?" Zack asked, hunkering down to study what they'd built.

"Yep. Dad says when I'm ten, I can saddle him myself. I won't just ride him. I'll take care of him, too."

"Josh. Come take your medicine," Mary Jo called from the kitchen.

The five-year-old turned up his nose.

Zack gently ruffled the boy's hair. "It'll make you feel better. Remember that when it's going down."

Struck again by how easily Zack related to Josh, she couldn't help but wonder what he'd done before he started riding across the country.

He rose to his feet and towered over her.

Lucy stood and found herself very close to Zack. He didn't move and neither did she.

Suddenly Rick burst in the door. "Has anyone seen Marty?"

Lucy took a deep breath. "I thought he was with you and Dad."

"Not since two. He went into Long Brush for a load of feed. But he should have been back by now."

"I mentioned I needed a few things at the tack shop. Maybe he stopped for them and saw someone he knew."

He's not answering his cell," Rick said.

"Maybe he stopped at Jerry's ranch. Cell coverage is spotty out there." She could always hope he'd simply gone to his friend's place for understanding and conversation before coming home.

"I'd better get back home. Mom might need help with supper." With a promise to call Rick if she heard from Marty, Lucy shrugged into her coat and pulled on her gloves. After a hug for Josh and good nights all around, she and Zack stepped outside.

As soon as they'd reached the split rail fence at the

end of the walk, Zack asked, "Do you have any idea where Marty is?"

"No, but I'm going to call around and see if I can find him." She just hoped he wasn't sitting on a bar stool at the Wooden Nickel.

"So you have an idea where he is. Why didn't you tell Rick what you suspect?"

"What do I suspect?"

"That he's holed up somewhere drinking."

"I don't know that."

Zack clasped her arm. "Lucy, let him handle the consequences of his actions."

As she tugged away, she heard the sound of a truck on gravel.

Marty roared up the lane in a cloud of dust.

Lucy breathed a sigh of relief. "There he is. Everything's fine."

"For the moment," Zack murmured.

Ignoring Zack's underlying message, Lucy ran by the corral and headed toward home. Zack was right beside her as she met her brother at the porch. "Rick was worried about you. Are you all right?"

Draping his arm around her shoulders, ignoring Zack, Marty assured her, "I'm fine. Just got tied up at the feed mill, that's all. I wish Rick would get off my back. The feed's in the truck safe and sound. I'll unload it after supper."

Although she couldn't smell alcohol, Lucy realized Marty was chewing gum. "I want you to look at Blazer if you have time."

"Blazer?"

"The new horse. Check his eyes for me. I think we have to do some doctoring."

"No problem. Maybe you should teach Zack, here, the veterinary points of running the place. He seems to be learning everything else."

"Marty…"

"I'll check him, Sis. Before I unload the truck. Let's go get some grub." He ushered her inside, effectively ending their conversation.

Blazer wouldn't let Marty get near him.

After supper Zack watched from outside the horse's stall as Lucy cooed and soothed and stroked. But Blazer kept shying away from Marty, dancing sideways, whinnying and pawing the ground.

Impatiently, Marty threw up his hands in exasperation and gave up, stepping into the walkway. "I don't know why you bother with animals like this."

"Because they need *someone* to bother with them. He's only been here a few days."

"Yeah, and it's going to be more than a few more before he's ready for anyone to handle him but you. You've got a pet, Lucy. A permanent one."

With that, Marty brushed by Zack and left the barn.

Lucy simply stroked Blazer.

Zack said, "It won't work, you know."

Her gaze swung toward him. "What won't work?"

"You trying to get Marty involved in life again.

He's a smart man. He could see what you're doing as well as I could. You didn't need him here to look at Blazer's eyes, did you?"

Lucy avoided his gaze. "I can always use a second opinion."

Zack approached the stall. With his gaze on the horse for signs of agitation, he stepped inside.

"Zack…" Lucy warned.

He moved slowly as the horse eyed him warily. Suddenly Blazer threw back his head and whinnied. Without retreating, Zack said, "Easy boy. It's okay. No one's going to hurt you."

The horse swished his tail.

With a slow and easy lift of his arm, Zack offered his hand to the horse.

Blazer sniffed, shook his head but didn't back away.

Smiling, Zack scratched the horse in back of his ears.

"You didn't tell me you were this good with animals," Lucy said softly.

"You didn't ask."

"Marty can usually handle the horses."

"They can feel hostility, even when it's not directed at them. Marty's angry. Even though he's taking it out on himself, this horse could still feel it."

Standing beside Zack, Lucy stroked Blazer's neck. "I don't know what to do for him."

"That's the problem, Lucy. *You* can't do anything. Marty has to help himself."

"I'm sorry he's so rude to you."

"You don't have to apologize for what he says and

does. Let him carry the responsibility himself." Zack could tell that concept bothered Lucy. Clasping her shoulder, he turned her toward him. "You're his sister, Lucy, not his keeper."

She looked up at him with wide brown eyes that melted his heart. "You don't understand."

"What don't I understand?"

"That Marty has always played and worked beside me. Rick was older and was usually off with Dad. But Marty…he never resented me taking the youngest's place. He always picked me up when I fell. When I was in…"

She stopped and Zack wondered what the thoughts were she wouldn't let escape.

"He's just always been there," she continued. "And I want to do the same for him."

Zack had never met someone as compassionate…as giving as Lucy. He'd loved his wife deeply, but as a lawyer she'd had a tough side that stood her well in the courtroom, but carried over into how she saw the world. Lucy saw her world differently, without cynicism and *with* hope. He felt guilty for comparing the two women, almost as guilty as he felt about wanting to kiss Lucy and hang the consequences.

When he bent his head, though, he didn't care about guilt as much as about the need racing through his body, the thrum of desire that had been frozen for so long. His first kiss with Lucy had awakened it. She was sweetness and caring and all the good he'd forgotten about or overlooked as he tried to distract himself from the past. His lips met hers this time with the fervor he thought he'd never feel again.

Go gently, he told himself. *Don't frighten her*. But as his lips moved over hers, "gentle" simply wasn't enough. Adrenaline pumped and he pulled her closer. Her jacket was in the way and so was his. Too much material…not enough of Lucy. He slipped his fingers along her nape…into her hair…and held her still as he slipped his tongue along the line of her lips.

Her soft gasp of surprise was all he needed. Passion flared hotter, insisting on more…more taste, more touch…more of sweetness and woman and Lucy. As he slid his fingers through her hair, he stroked his tongue against hers and felt her tremble. It was as if she'd never been kissed like this…as if she'd never known passion. He wanted to show her passion. He wanted to take her to Paradise and beyond.

At first Lucy didn't seem to know how to respond. But then her tongue tentatively touched his. He waited. She became bolder, teasing him, taunting him…with quick forays and inquisitive thrusts that drove him crazy.

Taking control again, he angled her head and pillaged her mouth while her hands grasped his shoulders. The same tension in him was driving her. He could feel it in her body moving against his, hear it in her soft moans of pleasure, taste it as their tongues mated.

Mated.

That's exactly where they were headed…toward a primal ritual that would be the worst mistake of his life and more important…hers.

With a bitter oath, he broke away. Where before Blazer had accepted his presence, now the horse sidestepped and pawed the hay.

Lucy's eyes still dazed with awakened desire, she reached for Blazer at the same time as Zack, their hands meeting on the horse's neck. What had come over her? The touch of Zack's lips had made her forget where she was. She'd never felt so on fire, so ready for something she didn't even know. But Zack had backed off, and looking at his remote expression now, she knew he'd keep backing off.

Yet she couldn't let him deny the feelings growing between them. "So that came from physical need, too?" she asked bluntly, keeping a soothing hand on Blazer as Zack moved away.

"Yes!" Zack exploded, not looking so remote any more. Then with his gaze colliding with hers, he shook his head. "Hell, I don't know where it came from. All I know is being around you is damn unsettling and I'm thinking about riding out of here before we do something we'll both regret."

In a way, that was quite an admission and filled Lucy with excitement. But in another, it was an insult. "You're acting as if I'd have no say in what happens."

"Judging from that kiss…"

"Maybe you shouldn't judge. Maybe I know better than you what the risks are." If they got more involved, she'd have to tell him she couldn't have children. Then he might ride out anyway. "If you want to leave, Zack, nothing's stopping you. We'll find another hand. So if you want to stay, stay. If you want to go, go. But don't blame either on *me*. Now, if you'll excuse me, I have to tend to Blazer. And the mood he's in, he might stomp on your foot."

Actually Blazer had calmed again, but Lucy hadn't. She held her breath as Zack took a last look at her and the horse…and then he walked away.

She told herself she should feel relieved.

But instead of feeling relieved, she just felt alone.

The sun was a brilliant ball defying the onset of winter as Zack carefully took Josh on a short run on his bike. When he returned, Lucy was standing beside Rick on the porch, looking on.

Zack hadn't spoken to her, at least nothing of any consequence, since their kiss in the barn. The next morning at breakfast, she'd arched a brow as if to say "so you're still here" and made polite conversation. It drove him crazy when she did that. Because whatever was on the surface with Lucy wasn't the end of it. There was a whole lot more. Yet the decision to get closer to her could hurt them both.

Watching her hug Josh after he finished his adventure, Zack knew he couldn't stay and not get closer. For a multitude of reasons, he felt led to stay, at least a little longer. And he hadn't felt led in a very long time.

He motioned to her. "C'mon. It's your turn. Let's go for a ride."

Her expression registered surprise and more than a little apprehension. Whether that came from the idea of riding a bike or holding onto him, he didn't know.

"I have to wash up and then help Mom with supper."

"You can come up with a better excuse than that,"

Zack teased. "If I didn't know better, I'd say you were afraid to try it."

Rick laughed. "I rode with Zack then took it out on my own. Josh just went for a spin and came back in one piece, too. I'm sure Zack will be careful with you. He'd have all of us to answer to if he's not."

Whether or not Rick's words were meant as a warning, Zack was aware of the underlying meaning and so was Lucy. After another moment's hesitation, she descended the porch steps and approached him slowly, almost as if he were a danger she wasn't ready to face.

He held out a helmet, one of two he'd ordered and had delivered yesterday. "I'll take it slow. C'mon. Put this on."

Taking the helmet from him, Lucy put it on and fastened the strap. Then she climbed on the bike behind him. He could tell she was hesitant to wrap her arms around him because she sat still for a moment.

"Put your arms around my waist, Lucy. And hold on."

When he started the bike, she wrapped her arms around him to steady herself. He liked the feeling of her behind him, her knees almost touching his thighs.

Then he zoomed off, entertaining the insane idea to ride off to nowhere...to everywhere...with Lucy behind him.

The roar of the wind against his helmet, its pull against his leather sleeves, couldn't distract him from Lucy's arms tightening around his waist. Is this why he'd insisted she ride with him? So he could feel her pressed against him?

That was part of the reason. But he also wanted to share the excitement and the sense of freedom. He could feel the tension leave her as she became more comfortable with the ride, more comfortable holding on to him.

Out on the main road, Zack appreciated the groves of pine trees, the birch and aspen, bare now, waiting for harsher weather. The land rolled by. Fence posts, too numerous to count, became a blurred border. The blue sky, open space, and ribbon of road invited Zack to keep on going and to never look back.

But he wasn't alone this time. His passenger had a life she loved on the Rising Star. Zack decreased his speed and pulled over to the shoulder. After checking for traffic, he made a U turn and headed back to the ranch. But instead of dropping Lucy at the house, he rode to the shed where he was storing his bike.

He waited until Lucy dismounted, then he climbed off. When she handed him her helmet, he hung it on the handlebar. Lifting his from his head, he asked, "Well, what did you think?"

"It's not so different from horseback riding."

"And you prefer a horse to a motorcycle," he joked.

"I didn't say that."

"You didn't have to." In just a short time, he felt he knew her.

"Why did you ask me to ride with you?"

"To try and give you a taste of my kind of freedom. So you'll understand."

"Why does it matter if I understand?"

Everything about her drew him toward her, away

from the bike and the freedom he thought he needed. "Lucy, I'm going to stay a few weeks and I'd like us to be friends."

"You could stay through the holidays."

"I could, but I don't know if I will." At her frown, he said, "Friends accept each other as they are."

Her eyes moved over his face and he stood very still, wondering what she was thinking, if she could accept his decision to leave when he felt he had to move on. Finally, she said, "I'd like to be your friend, Zack."

A sense of relief swept over him and he realized how important Lucy had become to him already. But it had been so long since he'd shut everyone not only out of his life, but out of his heart. Only Linc knew Zack's location. Thinking about his friend, Zack remembered the day he'd met the TV producer. Linc had been taping at the hospital where Zack had practiced. Over the years, they'd kept in touch in spite of work demands. Kay and Zack had often shared dinner out with Linc when their schedules allowed. Letting himself recall his life in L.A., Zack considered the rough patch in Linc's life and listening when Linc had needed to vent. After Zack had lost Kay, Linc had been there for him in the same way. Whenever Zack thought of Linc now, he had to smile because he knew Linc was gloriously happy with Emma and her little girl Becky.

Any day now, Zack should be hearing from him. Linc was a good friend. Zack knew Lucy could be a good friend, too. But did he simply want friendship from her?

When the wind teased her hair, Zack couldn't help but catch a strand of it. Wrapping the wave around his finger, he asked, "How about going into Long Brush with me Saturday night and catching a movie?"

The smile that broke over her face warmed every part of Zack that was cold. "I'd like that."

There was no pretense in Lucy. Another quality he admired. With her hair around his finger, he gently tugged her toward him knowing better than to tempt either one of them into an untenable situation while living under the same roof. He kissed her forehead. It wasn't nearly enough—her soft skin against his lips, the lightning flash of heat that speared through him, her hair against his finger—but it was all he would allow himself. It was all he could allow himself if he wanted to stay.

When he leaned away, he saw that she understood. If they became more than friends, he'd have to leave.

A few more weeks, Zack had said. *Maybe until Christmas*, Lucy hoped as she freshened up after a long work day on Friday. Tomorrow night, she and Zack would be going on a date. Only he probably wouldn't call it that.

As she pulled a fresh cotton blouse out of her closet to wear with clean jeans, she realized today had been different from all the others since Zack first arrived. They'd worked side by side mucking out stalls, grooming the horses, working the young stock. Zack had a way with animals. But although they'd agreed to be "friends," tension still hummed between them, especially when they got within a foot of each other. She could sense when he was watching her. The hairs on her neck would prickle.

Slipping on a pair of moccasins, she told herself not to get excited about tomorrow night. As she opened her top dresser drawer for a lip gloss, she spotted the picture she had slid along the side of the drawer. She'd memorized it—every feature on the two baby girls' faces, the edging on the pink blankets, the pompom on their little hats. More than once this week, she'd picked up her phone to call John Buckley. But then—

She'd run through the pros and cons again and had felt panic. She wasn't sure exactly why.

With a last look at the two babies, Lucy plucked her lip gloss from the drawer then carefully put the picture back in. After pulling a brush through her hair, she took a last look in the mirror, applied the lip gloss and hurried downstairs. She heard Zack's voice in the kitchen and headed that way. At the doorway their gazes met.

"I have to get cleaned up—" he started to say when suddenly a beeping came from his pocket. His cell phone. Zack's face showed no sense of surprise or any other emotion. He took his phone from his pocket and moved out of earshot into the living room.

Lucy was sorry about that because she was curious who was calling him. She'd like to overhear every word.

Zack answered the call. He'd picked up the pay-as-you-go phone when he'd started traveling, leaving his old cell phone and his pager back in Los Angeles.

"It's Linc."

"I figured as much," Zack said with a smile in his voice. "What's up?"

"The settlement went through on your condo. The funds are in your checking account."

Zack had given Linc power of attorney for just this reason. "Thanks. That should hold me for a long while."

"So exactly where are you this week?"

"Long Brush, Wyoming. A ranch called the Rising Star."

"How long are you going to stay?"

"Maybe till mid December. These are nice folks. They're going to be short-handed after Thanksgiving while one of the brothers takes horses to a cutting event in Fort Worth for a week."

"It sounds as if you're getting involved."

Zack heard the hopefulness in his friend's voice. "I'll be moving on again."

"Don't you think it's time you came back to your practice?"

"I don't have a practice. I sold it."

"You know what I mean. Come back to practicing medicine, Zack. You're too good to let your skills go to waste."

"I have other skills, too, remember? Roping and cutting and putting in a hard day's work so I can sleep at night."

"Zack…"

"Give it up, Linc. I don't know if I'll ever go back to it. I couldn't save the one person who mattered to me the most. What's the point?"

"You can help heal others. With your diagnostic skills, you belong in medicine."

"I belong where I can find a little bit of peace."

"And you've found it there?"

"Enough to keep me here for a while."

"So open an office there."

"Handle my finances for me, Linc. And leave the rest."

The silence showed his friend's disapproval. Since Linc was a good friend, Zack asked, "So how are Emma and Becky?"

Linc had been married shortly before Christmas last year. Since Linc was a media mogul and had been a long-time bachelor, Zack had been surprised when he'd fallen for a pretty single mom. But Linc had always wanted to be a family man. Unusual circumstances had brought him and Emma together and they'd both fallen hard before they'd realized it. Zack had met Emma and liked her. He hoped his friend would be truly happy.

"They're good. Emma's gift basket business is thriving with the holidays and Becky's all excited about Christmas. Her first grade Thanksgiving pageant is next week." Linc paused for a moment, then said, "I still can't believe I found Emma. She's— Well, you know."

Zack also knew Linc didn't want to rub his newfound happiness into Zack's old wounds. He advised Linc, "Enjoy every minute of it." He didn't have to add, *Because you never know when it might end.*

When Linc didn't respond, Zack knew there was understanding between them.

Finally, Linc said, "I don't know if you're crazy or

courageous giving up an old life and starting a new one. Take care of yourself, Zack."

"I will. And thanks. You're a good friend."

When Zack hung up the phone, he headed for the stairs. Maybe a shower would help wash away the sense of restlessness that talking to Linc always gave him. Reality was the Rising Star…here…now. The past was a memory. And the future?

The future was a ghost as unreal as the past.

Zack emerged from the bathroom in jeans, his hair damp. All he had to do was grab a shirt from his room…

Suddenly Lucy came toward him in the dim hall. The scent of lilacs hit him. Her hair was silky along her cheek, her lips a pretty pink.

"Supper's ready," she said.

As a doctor, Zack had worked out when he could to keep himself physically fit. As he'd traveled, the construction work and ranch chores had kept him in shape. He'd never thought much about his body, though Kay had teased him that he should pose for a calendar. He hadn't thought about that in a really long time.

Standing before Lucy now, he wasn't sure what he felt as her gaze dropped to his chest and he found himself getting turned on.

"I'll be ready in a minute." His voice came out low and husky.

Her gaze finally found his. "I…uh…wondered if

the phone call was anything important. I mean an emergency or something."

"It wasn't."

"And everything's all right?"

"Everything's fine."

She obviously wasn't getting the answers she wanted because she pressed, "Then you're not leaving sooner than you expected."

"No. I told your father today that I'd stay until after Rick gets back from Fort Worth."

"I see."

He couldn't help moving closer to her, wanting to take her in his arms and kiss her silly. Restraining the urge, trying to keep emotional space between them if not physical, he said, "I told you I value my privacy."

"Yes, you did. But you also gave me the impression you have no ties anywhere. And with that phone call…"

"I have no ties, Lucy. And I gave your dad my word I'd stay until mid-December. Take it for what it's worth."

Her eyes widened and she looked hurt for a moment.

His gut clenched.

But then she said, "I think your word is worth a lot." Without giving him a chance to respond, she turned away from him and headed for the kitchen.

"Lucy?"

Stopping, she stood in the archway and waited.

"We're still on for tomorrow night. Unless you've changed your mind."

"I haven't changed my mind. We can take my car if you'd like."

"Don't want to zip into town on a Harley?" he teased.

"The temperature's supposed to drop tonight. We might be more comfortable in a car."

Comfortable. In a darkened car. With Lucy beside him. He just wouldn't take any detours or end up on Lover's Lane.

Chapter Five

"Lucy, we're leaving," Esther called up the stairs Saturday evening. "It might be late till we get back. You know what happens when your father and Wes get to talking."

Pulling her bedroom door open, Lucy went to stand at the top of the steps. "Have fun." Her parents played cards with their neighbors whenever they could.

Lucy's mother looked up at her from the bottom step. "Zack's waiting."

"Tell him I'll be down in a few minutes." After she'd come in from the barn, she'd eaten supper, then showered. Her indecision about what to wear had put her behind schedule. She'd finally decided on a violet silky blouse and black slacks. Hurrying back to her room, she dabbed perfume on her wrists and behind her ears.

When she came down the steps, Zack was sitting on the sofa reading the newspaper. He looked up, and Lucy's heart almost stopped. Something about that look in his eyes made her tingle from head to toe, but she kept putting one foot in front of the other.

He stood with a grimace. "I thought jeans would work for the movies."

She couldn't imagine him looking any finer than he did in the grey western-cut shirt and black denims. "Jeans do work. I just thought I'd take the opportunity to dress up a little."

His gaze traveled up and down her silky sleeves...over the rest of her. Raking his hand through his hair, he said, "We should be going."

She approached him slowly, both excited and a little afraid of the sparks in his eyes. "I'd like to know something first."

"What?"

"Why did you ask me to the movies tonight?"

"I thought you'd like to get off the ranch for a while."

"That's all?" She knew she was pushing. But she could no longer deny the pull toward Zack and she had to know where she stood.

"I want to spend some time with you...in a safe setting," he admitted.

"Safe?"

"Let me put it this way, Lucy. We're alone now. Here. But if we stayed, you might not be safe."

"I'd be safe with you."

With a bittersweet smile, he shook his head. "If you knew my thoughts right now, you'd head back upstairs and lock your door."

His words sent a shiver up her spine. "You seem so sure about what I'd do. You might be wrong."

The air between them simmered with what might happen...what could happen if they gave in to the pull between them. Zack reached for her, pulling her into his arms. As he bent his head, the phone rang.

Lucy waited, but his lips never touched hers. Instead, he said, "You'd better get that."

The phone rang again.

Stilling the trembling that had begun the moment Zack had touched her, Lucy picked up the receiver. "McIntyres."

"Lucy, is that you?" a gruff voice asked.

"Yes—"

"It's Bud. At the Wooden Nickel. Marty's sloshed. Almost got into a brawl. And I've got his keys. No way he's drivin' home. What do you want me to do?"

The hope Lucy had nurtured for the past week that her brother was finally getting back his old perspective wilted. "I'll be there as soon as I can. See if you can keep him there."

"He's not goin' nowhere. Leastways, not on his own steam. I'll see if I can get some coffee in him."

"Thanks, Bud." When she hung up, she turned to Zack.

"To the rescue again?" he asked with an arched brow.

His attitude rankled. He had no right to judge how she handled her brother. "This has never happened before."

"No? Well, you can be sure it will happen again if you charge in and fix it."

"What am I supposed to do? Leave him stranded?

Or worse yet, let him convince Bud to give him back his keys? I don't think so."

"So our night gets shot to hell."

The cold-edged anger in Zack's voice made her realize she was making a choice that would affect what was growing between them. "Zack, I'm sorry."

"No, I don't think you are. This problem of Marty's makes you feel needed and you like that."

"What an *awful* thing to say! I don't know how you were raised, but Mom and Dad taught us to help each other, to stand by each other, to never let each other down. It's called loyalty and it's part of my being Marty's sister."

"And I think you're a little too willing to help. Everyone. All the time. You have no life of your own. Your world revolves around your family. They adopted you, Lucy, but that doesn't mean you owe them gratitude for the rest of your life. It doesn't mean you have to give them your soul."

Lucy felt as if Zack had slapped her, as if any closeness they'd felt had been a mirage. She didn't know this man who wanted her to turn her back on the people she held most dear. Before the hurt and anger welled into tears, she spun around and headed for the closet. As she snatched her wool poncho from a hanger, she felt Zack behind her. He pulled his jacket from the closet, too.

She didn't care where he was going. She just knew she had to get away from him and get to her brother. But as she walked to the garage, he was right beside her.

Over her shoulder, she asked, "What do you think you're doing?"

"I'm coming with you. You might not be able to handle him yourself."

Throwing the lock, she said, "I'll be just fine. I don't want you involved when it's the last thing you want to do."

"Well, I am involved. I was here when the call came. And somebody has to drive Marty's truck. So why don't we just call this a payback for your family's hospitality and be done with it."

Zack climbed into the car and waited for her. Even angrier because she knew she just might *need* his help, she pulled open the driver's door and slid inside.

It was a cold, silent ride as the wind picked up and whistled against the vehicle. But she felt much colder inside. Exactly what did she know about Zackary Burke? A few hot kisses and she'd thought she was falling in love.

In love?

The words struck fear in her.

Zack was a wanderer and apparently he didn't know the first thing about being a member of a family. Reason told her she could never fall in love with a man like that who didn't have the same values, who didn't understand that a family was a person's protection against the world.

The Wooden Nickel sat on Main Street in Long Brush two doors up from the pharmacy and two doors down from the bank. She'd only been inside once before, when her brothers had taken her there for her first drink on her twenty-first birthday. It had been a ritual she'd always remember, not necessarily an experience she'd want to repeat. Cars lined the curb and she had to park a block away. Neither she nor Zack spoke as they walked to the front door of the saloon.

As soon as she opened the heavy wooden door, she grudgingly had to admit she was glad Zack was beside her. The sound of the sports channel on the TV hit her first. Trying to block it out, she wove through the lodge pine tables and chairs, trying to ignore the feeling of many eyes on her. Most of the customers wore boots and Stetsons and tonight she felt out of place.

When she stopped for a moment to get her bearings, a man at the table by her left gave a loud wolf whistle. "Ain't seen the likes of you here before," he called over the TV.

Suddenly, Zack was at her side, clasping her elbow. "Not likely you will again," he called back as he guided her with his large hand in the center of her back. The imprint burned through her poncho.

Not one barstool stood empty. After all, it was Saturday night. Bud saw her and motioned to the last stool at the bar in the darkest corner. When Lucy glanced in the immense tavern mirror, she saw Zack's scowl.

Spinning around, she said, "I can do this myself. If you want to wait outside—"

"I'm here. Let's get this over with."

She could hardly hear herself think, let alone have an argument with Zack. Standing behind her brother, she put her hand on his shoulder. "Marty?"

He turned slowly, as if he couldn't figure out where he was or who would be calling his name. "Lu…Lucy. Zat you?"

"Yes, it's me. I've come to take you home. Can you walk?"

He tried to stand and nearly fell from the stool. "Sure, I can walk."

Zack stepped in and hoisted Marty up. "Okay, hotshot. Let's go. We ought to sit you on the hood of the car so you get some fresh air." He glanced at Lucy. "But your sister would think that's cruel and unusual punishment. Try to put one foot in front of the other."

All Lucy could do to help was lead the way. When she opened the door, the blast of wind hit her. Once outside, she waited until Zack made his way to the curb where Marty's truck was parked. "I need his keys," Zack growled.

"I have a spare set. Put him in my car and I'll give them to you."

"You might not be able to handle him."

"I can handle him if you just get him to my car."

As she'd asked, Zack supported Marty until they reached Lucy's car. Then none too gently, he dumped him in, buckled the seatbelt and slammed the door. "I'll follow you. If he acts up, pull over."

"He's had too much to drink. He's not going to go wild on me."

"Just play it safe, Lucy," Zack said sternly. "For your sake and his."

Apparently underneath Zack's exasperation with her was a concern for her welfare. If only they'd had tonight together. "Any problems and I'll pull over. I promise."

Zack held her gaze for a moment, then said tersely, "I'll see you back at the ranch."

Marty fell asleep in the car, mumbling every now and then. She heard Angie's name and couldn't make out anything else. Instead of driving to the garage, she pulled up in front of the house. It was dark so she knew her parents hadn't yet come home.

Zack pulled up in back of her. Before she could even exhale a sigh of relief, he was at the passenger door.

Lucy ran ahead, opened the door to the house, and switched the lights on. Out of habit, she hung her car keys on the line of hooks by the closet door.

Supporting Marty, Zack hoisted him up the stairs. "Which room?"

"Second on the right."

By the time Zack ungraciously dropped Marty on the bed, her brother groaned and held his head.

Lucy sank down beside him. "I'll get you a couple of aspirin and a pot of coffee."

"Forget the coffee," Zack said from his position at the doorway. "That will only dehydrate him. Get as much water into him as you can. Juice won't hurt. There's no quick fix for being drunk."

Zack's voice was filled with the same authority she'd heard when he'd checked Josh's throat. But before she could question him, he said, "I'll put your car and the truck in the garage."

"I know where your keys are. I'll put them back when I'm finished."

Wanting to thank him for his help, but knowing he was upset with her, she let him go.

After Lucy had taken Marty a water pitcher and a glass of juice and made sure he drank some of both, she sat at the foot of the bed. "If you come home like this again, Mom and Dad will find out."

"Stuff the lecture, okay? My head's hammering too bad. I jus' got a little soused."

"A little?"

"Lucy, I jus' want to sleep."

"I'll let you sleep now if you promise to talk to me about this in the morning."

"Fine. In the mornin'." Lying back, he crossed one boot over the other and threw his arm across his forehead.

There was no way she could get through to him now. But in the morning, she'd try to convince him to get some help...from *someone*.

Deciding she had to see Zack before she went to her room, she checked the first floor. His bedroom door was open and he was nowhere in sight. Drawn to the kitchen door, she looked out. Zack stood by the porch post backlit by the moon. Hesitating only a moment, she stepped outside.

He didn't turn, just stared out and up, above the pines, to the mountains. Even with the full moon, shapes dissolved into shadows and the black sky almost touched the earth. As clouds slipped across the expanse with the gusts of wind, only a few stars shone through the film.

"I'm sorry our plans were disrupted tonight." Her voice rang clear as the night seemed to stand still.

"Are you, Lucy? Or was Marty a convenient excuse to keep you from facing what's going on with us?"

"If you remember, I was ready to face it. I didn't arrange that phone call."

Zack turned toward her then. "No, I suppose you didn't. And it was just as well it came. Neither of us is ready to deal with more than anticipation and a bit of excitement."

She knew he was just passing through. More than anything, she wanted to ask him to stay, to tell him she couldn't have children, to explore the attraction. But they hadn't known each other long enough or well enough to ask, or explain, or even to kiss without feeling as if they were stepping over some kind of forbidden line. Was she attracted to Zack *because* he was unattainable? Because he was a nomad and he was more of a fantasy than a reality?

Difficult questions she needed to answer before anything else happened between them...before the next kiss led to regrets.

Zack had stated the reality and she couldn't refute it. He was holding in so much...she could feel it. And if he wanted to keep escaping his grief and pain, there was nothing she could do.

"Thank you for your help with Marty. If you hadn't been here..."

"It might have been better for him."

"Zack—"

He shook his head. "I've said enough on the subject. It's closed. He's your brother. But the more you both deny what's happening, the longer it'll go on." As the wind lifted her hair and blew it along her cheek, he said, "You'd better go in. I'm going to check the horses."

"You don't have to. Rick usually makes a last round when he knows Dad's not here."

"I'm restless, Lucy. I need to move around. And I need to put some distance between me and you. Go on inside before we pick up where we left off before the phone rang."

The last thing she wanted to do was go into the house. But tonight, she'd take Zack's advice. Maybe tomorrow morning when the sun came up, she could see more clearly.

Zack watched her as she moved away and opened the door. When she stepped over the threshold and closed it behind her, she heard his boots on the porch steps and the sound drifting away.

Lucy had just finished dressing Sunday morning when there was a slight rap on her bedroom door. When she opened it, she wasn't surprised to see Marty. "How are you feeling?" she asked, motioning him inside.

"Like a herd of wild stallions galloped through my head. Damn, I was stupid last night."

Taking the tactful route, she said nothing.

"Did I imagine it, or was Burke with you at the Wooden Nickel?"

"He was with me. And a good thing, too. I don't think I could have handled you on my own."

"I hate being beholden to a stranger."

"Zack's no stranger."

With a protective brother's interest, he asked, "Is something going on between you two?"

Lucy sank down on the bed. "I'm not sure."

Slowly, as if each step gave him a worse headache, Marty sat beside her. "Be careful, Luce."

Closer to Marty than Rick, mainly because they were closer in age, she'd always confided in him. "When you pass a certain point, I'm not sure anyone can really *be* careful."

"Are you past that point?"

She knew he was genuinely interested, but she also knew he was trying to keep the conversation away from what had happened at the Wooden Nickel. "Are *you*?"

"Angie and I are finished."

"That's not what I mean. A drink now and then is one thing, Marty. Regularly and to numb yourself so you don't think about anything is something else."

"We've had this conversation before. I didn't come in here for a lecture."

"Why did you come in?"

"To thank you."

"And?" she pressed.

"Dammit, Lucy, you know me too well. You're not going to tell Mom and Dad, are you?"

"I won't lie to them."

"But you won't volunteer information, either, will you? Come on, Luce, cover for me. I don't want to worry them."

"Is there anything for them to worry about?"

He couldn't meet her gaze. Pushing himself from the bed, he went and stood at her window looking out over the firs and cottonwoods. "I won't let last night happen again. I promise."

They didn't lie to each other. "All right. I won't say anything. But I can't speak for Zack."

"He'll keep quiet."

"What makes you think so?"

"He's got his own secrets."

"You know something in particular?"

"No. But a grown man doesn't ride around the country with no good reason. Not a man like him. Watch out. I don't want to see you get hurt."

"I don't want to see *you* get hurt, either. If you need help—"

"I'm *fine*. I told you, last night won't happen again. I've got to get out to the barn. I told Dad I'd groom the mares. I can do that, even with this damn headache." He strode to the door and stopped at the threshold. "Thanks for last night. I know I can count on you. That means a lot."

What could she say to that?

As Marty closed the door, she became hopeful again that he really was going to get his life back on track.

Dusty and tired, but edgy enough to want to climb on his bike and hit the road, Zack snatched his Stetson from his head on Monday evening and ran his fingers through his hair. Even physical labor couldn't make him forget Lucy. He couldn't help but wonder what would have happened if the phone hadn't rung Saturday night before their date.

Some date.

Yet maybe the fates knew better than he what was

best for him. At least this time. The point was he knew he couldn't fight fate or defy it, but sometimes it was damn hard to accept it.

The light from the kitchen in the almost-dark beckoned to him. This house was a symbol of everything a home should be. His chest tightened as he wondered if Lucy was still working in the barn or arena or if he'd find her inside.

When he opened the kitchen door, the smells of supper wound about him, drawing him in. But instead of Esther standing at the counter, he found Lucy! She was kneading some sort of dough in a deep ceramic bowl.

"Taking over for your mom?" he asked casually.

"She spilled beet juice on her blouse and went to change. I told her I'd make the biscuits."

Lucy looked just-right wrist-deep in dough and he could imagine her cooking with kids hanging out around her in the kitchen.

"What?" she asked as he realized he was still staring at her.

Crossing to her, he brushed his thumb across a streak of flour on her cheek and smiled. "You wear your flour well."

Her hands stopped kneading, and her eyes sparkled in the kitchen light. He could feel her anticipation as well as his own, an anticipation that was becoming as hard to resist as she was. Well…almost.

A truck rolled to a stop outside. A few seconds later, there came a sharp rap on the door. Since he was closer to it, Zack opened it. The delivery man handed him a box and, after a courteous smile, left.

Zack glanced at the package. "It's for you."

From the expression on Lucy's face as she washed and dried her hands, she'd expected it. She tried to open the box but the flap was stubborn.

Zack took it from her and slipped his hand into his jeans for his pocket knife.

Lucy studied the knife for a few moments then asked, "Can I see that?"

He handed it over, knowing why she'd asked. "The handle is elk bone, dyed with blueberries," he offered. Then he added, "My father gave it to me when I turned sixteen." Now why had he added that?

Examining it, Lucy saw that it had three blades that were all sharp. "You take good care of it." Her gaze met his, asking for more personal information. But he'd already said enough. Pulling out the largest blade, he made quick work of the flap on her package and handed it back to her.

She started to pull the books out of the box, then hesitated. "I might as well run this upstairs to my room."

"Contraband material?" he joked.

Lucy lowered her voice. "Books about twins."

"You haven't ruled out finding your sister."

Her eyes troubled, she shook her head. "With Thanksgiving next week, I've been thinking about her even more."

Zack nodded to the box in her hand. "What do you think you'll find there?"

"Direction, maybe guidance. Maybe just a feeling that I'm doing the right thing if I start a search. I don't know. I want to read about the connection, bonds. It's about twins separated from birth."

"There are lots of studies, Lucy, but no study is going to settle it for you."

She was looking at him curiously. "How do you know there are lots of studies?"

As a doctor, he'd read more journals than he could ever count. But just like the normal population, he knew twins were a hot topic in the nurture versus nature debate. "I watch TV specials now and then. I read."

Her gaze searched his and he felt uncomfortable for a moment.

"Zack, there are so many things I don't know about you."

"I imagine there's a lot I don't know about you."

He noticed the pulse beating rapidly at her throat. Then her eyes dropped to the package in her hand. "I'm going to take this upstairs. Supper will be ready in about a half hour."

He'd gotten good at fielding questions, at turning them around. It usually worked. The problem was as Lucy climbed the stairs, he doubted if he'd let any woman really know him ever again.

Chapter Six

It was after midnight. Zack cut himself a piece of lemon meringue pie and sat at the table in the kitchen with a crossword puzzle magazine he'd found in the living room. Taking a ball point pen from his shirt pocket—as a doctor he'd carried one out of habit to write a prescription or make notes on a chart—he studied the first blank puzzle. Staring at the ceiling with his eyes open was getting to be an exercise in frustration. He'd told himself he was hungry and that the pie would help him get to sleep, but he knew it wasn't hunger for pie that kept him awake.

When he heard Lucy on the stairs, he looked up. She stopped when she saw him, hesitated a moment but then descended the remainder of the steps. She was wearing her pink chenille robe again. Her hair was slightly tousled and he wondered if she'd been tossing and turning, too. He'd pulled on his jeans and flannel shirt but his feet were bare and the coldness of the linoleum under them was a contrast against the heat he felt whenever he looked at Lucy.

"Sleepwalking?" he asked with a smile, trying to keep the atmosphere light.

"I wish it were as simple as that," she said, not returning his smile. She looked troubled and he pushed his pie away, giving her his full attention.

"What's the matter?"

Her gaze drifted down his open shirt and she didn't come any closer. "I can't lay my problems on you."

"You don't have to. I can just listen." Being a doctor of internal medicine had taught him how to listen well. Often it was what a patient said even more than the physical symptoms that helped him diagnose the problem.

Still hesitating, she went to the stove and picked up a tea kettle then filled it with water. "I read the books that came."

"And what did you learn?"

After she turned off the water spigot, she set the tea pot on the stove.

"That maybe I'm not a twin. I've never felt a psychic connection to someone else."

"Whoa!" he said. "That doesn't mean you're not a twin. Besides, does it matter if you have a twin or just a sister?"

"She wouldn't be just a sister."

"What would she be?" he asked quietly.

"My only living relative."

"Lucy, why don't you talk to your mother about this?"

She switched on the burner under the teapot. "I can't. My family's given me everything. I can't betray them by looking for more love."

"Betrayal is a funny word to use. Why do you feel it would be betraying them?"

She shrugged. "I can't explain it. Why should I want more?"

He stood and approached her slowly. Standing in front of her, he stared at her intently. "Listen to me, Lucy, you can never have too much love. You can never appreciate it enough. If you have a sister, you deserve to know her and she deserves to know you. Maybe she doesn't have the family you have. Did you ever think of that?"

He noticed the confusion in Lucy's eyes as she admitted, "No, I didn't."

Her robe had opened slightly and dipped to a V at her waist. The cotton nightgown underneath had narrow blue stripes and white trim around the neck that led to three buttons at her breast. When he looked at those buttons, he could only think of doing one thing with them.

"Think about sharing your life with someone else, Lucy. Maybe even sharing your family. That's a gift your sister might appreciate."

"It's a gift she might not want."

"But you're not going to know unless you search for her and find her, are you?"

They gazed at each other for what seemed like a very long time. Lucy lifted her chin slightly and he stepped even closer until her robe brushed his jeans. He grazed her cheek with the back of his knuckles. "There's something about being alone down here with you at night."

"What kind of something?" she asked breathlessly.

He shook his head as if trying to deny it, but then he couldn't and his lips dipped to hers. Their melding was sweet. He moved his mouth over hers and nibbled slightly, then resting there and prolonging each moment of sensation. He was about to do much more when the tea kettle whistled.

Turning away from him, she swiftly turned off the burner. "I'll have everybody awake," she murmured.

"You definitely have *me* awake."

When she swung around to look at him, her color was high. "Would you like to go out with me Friday night?"

Her question surprised him. "Go out?"

"I want to make up to you for the other night. I promise nothing will interfere this time."

He knew he shouldn't. He knew he should stay away from her. He knew he wasn't ready for what might happen if he didn't. Yet he didn't think Lucy was the type to be forward and he wondered why she was being more forward than he'd expected now. "What do you have in mind?"

"There's a country-western place on the outskirts of Long Brush. They have a band on Friday and Saturday nights. Do you like to dance?"

"I haven't done a lot of it, but I'm game."

"They teach new-comers a basic line dance, so you can get into the swing of it pretty quickly."

"It's not really dancing unless you're holding a woman in your arms," he teased.

"You don't strike me as a traditionalist," she responded.

"You'd be surprised at just how traditional I am."

"Maybe I wouldn't be. Just because you ride a Harley doesn't mean you belong on one."

Lucy's perceptiveness always struck him as too insightful for a woman as young as she was. "I belong on whatever gets me where I want to go."

"And where do you want to go?"

"Right now, I guess to bed." He didn't say "with her" and he didn't say "to do more than sleep" because if he said it, it might just become reality.

Squaring her shoulders and belting her robe tighter, Lucy asked, "And about Friday night?"

Since he rode a Harley as well as a horse, he had to fulfill an image—an image that said he could handle anything, go anywhere, take any risk. "You're on for Friday night, but I expect to dance at least one dance holding you in my arms. Deal?"

"Deal," she agreed with a shy smile that made him think about consequences rather than risks.

As Zack and Lucy entered the Long Brush Corral, he could see the honky-tonk catered to anyone who wanted to listen to heart-true music and have a good time. The wooden tables and chairs looked as old as the town. The mirror along the long bar reflected Stetsons as well as name-brand beers. There wasn't a spare seat when Zack and Lucy arrived around nine o-clock on Friday. But there were still empty tables and he showed her to one, then glanced at the band in the back with it's yard-high speakers. High-tech seemed incongruous with the rest of the old-west atmosphere. Several people nodded to Lucy and said hello. A few of them were men, and Zack wondered if she'd dated any of them. He felt a swell of jealousy when he thought about it and knew the feeling wasn't appropriate. Yet it was there anyway.

As Lucy unbuttoned her poncho, he stood behind her and helped her out of it. His fingers brushed her arm and she glanced at him over her shoulder. They'd both been quiet on the ride to Long Brush, and he'd kicked himself for giving in to what seemed like almost a dare from her. He was playing with fire and he knew it, but the numbness that he'd felt for so long seemed to be diminishing with each passing day. That had to do with Lucy's warmth and the heat that flared between them. Maybe getting burned would make him feel alive again. Maybe getting burned would be better than not feeling anything at all.

When a waitress came to their table and asked what they'd like to drink, they both ordered sodas. Lucy said, "I can drive home if you want to have something."

He shook his head. "I don't think I should mix alcohol and line dancing. Somebody could get hurt."

She laughed, and he loved the sound of it. "Surely you don't have two left feet."

"We'll find out shortly," he said grinning back at her. When she leaned forward across the table, her knee brushed his and he didn't move away.

"Where did you go to school, Zack?"

"How do you know I did?"

"You're well-educated. It's obvious, even if you don't want it to be."

"I might have to let my hair grow, buy leather slacks and get a few tattoos to go with my Harley," he grumbled.

"If you don't want to tell me, you don't have to. I was just curious."

"I went to Stanford."

"Stanford? Wow! Are you from California?"

"Yes, I am."

She crossed one hand over the other. "That seems like a world away."

"It is."

Before her curiosity took her into territory where he'd rather not venture, he asked, "Do you come here often?" There seemed to be a lot of singles sitting, talking, milling about, and he imagined it was a good place to hook up with someone.

"No. Just once in a while."

"Do you come alone?"

"With friends."

"Any one friend in particular?"

She shook her head and looked relieved when the waitress brought their drinks. By then the music had started up and lines already formed across the dance floor. One of the members of the band told newcomers to come right on up and learn a few steps so they could join in the fun.

Lucy tilted her head at him. "Are you ready?"

"As ready as I'm going to be." Then he stood and escorted her to the lines that were forming.

For the next half-hour Zack tried to learn steps that seemed as complicated as any innovative medical procedure. But as his feet tangled and he bumped into Lucy, laughed and enjoyed just being with her, he finally got the hang of most of the routine. They danced a few dances after that and he was surprised at how well he did.

At the end of one of the songs, Lucy clasped his arm. "You've finally gotten the hang of it."

The admiration and respect in her voice, the way she was looking at him, urged him to ask, "How about some drinks before we tackle the next set."

For a while they sat munching peanuts and sipping sodas. Lucy was wearing dress jeans tonight and a soft pink sweater with a fine gold chain around her neck. Her cheeks were full of color and her eyes sparkled.

"Dancing becomes you," he remarked.

She looked flustered for a moment, then murmured, "Thank you," and took a few more sips of her soda. Everything about her told him she wasn't experienced with men and he wondered why not.

When the band started up again, the music was sweeter, softer, slower, and he knew this was why he had come tonight. This was the dance he wanted to dance with her.

"Ready for more?" he asked, as if dancing to the ballad would be no different than dancing in a line of people that stretched across the room.

When she nodded, he stood and offered her his hand. She took it. On the dance floor, he drew her into his arms slowly and then relished the feel of having her there. Closing his fingers over hers, he brought her hand into his chest and held her. Her lilac perfume filled his lungs and the desire to do more than dance made him aware of the creamy texture of her skin, the softness of her hair as he brushed it from her shoulder, the enticing curve of her lips. Other couples toured the floor around them, but he felt as if the two of them were suspended, moving in their own dimension, dancing to music meant only for them. Lucy filled his mind and his arms and his world, and he couldn't imagine being anywhere else. She moved so easily with him, following him, as if she'd been doing it for years.

Their first dance blended into a second and he held her even closer. His jaw brushed her cheek. It felt so good he did it again. She seemed to snuggle into him and his lips grazed her temple. When she looked up at him, he became fully aroused. Her eyes widened but he didn't put space between them and she didn't pull away. It was sweet torture feeling her against him, yet knowing nothing could happen here—nothing more than a light kiss, unless they wanted to make spectacles of themselves. He'd never do that to her.

When the dance ended, he couldn't help brushing his lips over hers. As he raised his head, she smiled at him and he almost groaned. So much for a chaste kiss. He was as primed as if they'd been necking for an hour.

But as he led her from the dance floor, she suddenly stopped cold. They were practically face to face with another couple.

The man shifted from one foot to the other, looking awkward. "Hi, Lucy."

"Hello, Pete."

The man was blond with brown eyes, good-looking, and Zack disliked him on sight. He also didn't need an explanation to suspect Lucy had dated this man or been more than a little involved.

The man named Pete wrapped his arm around the woman's waist who was standing beside him and said, "Lucy, this is Marjorie. Marjorie Wilson."

The woman nodded and smiled. "Soon to be Marjorie Cantrell," she added.

Lucy's eyes went to the ring on the woman's finger. It was large and flashy. "Congratulations," she said with a smile that Zack could tell was forced. Then she turned to him. "This is Zackary Burke."

"Oh. You're the new hand on the Rising Star," Cantrell commented. "I heard Lucy's dad had hired someone. Good to meet you."

Pete Cantrell made "hired hand" sound like a dirty word. Zack inclined his head slightly and draped his arm around Lucy's shoulders and pulled her closer. "We'd better get back to our table before we lose it. It's getting more crowded in here."

After a few exchanged "good-byes" and "nice-to-see-you's" they crossed to their table. Lucy avoided his eyes for a few moments, then finally looked at him.

"We can go whenever you'd like," she said.

He wasn't going to pretend as if nothing had happened. "I don't want to leave. But if you don't want to be in the same room with Pete Cantrell, we can. I'd like to know why, though."

"It doesn't bother me to be in the same room with him," she said a little too decisively.

"Who is he?"

"An accountant."

"I didn't ask what he *did*, I asked who he was to you."

"What makes you think you have the right to know?"

"The way we were dancing on the dance floor."

That must have struck a chord because she told him some of what he wanted to know. "We dated for a while."

"Seriously?"

"Yes."

"What happened?"

"It doesn't matter what happened, Zack. It's over. Pete and I went our separate ways."

"Are you sure it's over?"

"Oh, I'm very sure. From the look of that ring on Marjorie Wilson's finger, Pete is, too."

"Maybe he's still not carrying a torch, but are you?"

She shook her head vehemently. "No. Pete's not the kind of man I thought he was."

Lucy was the type of woman who would want a hero or prince, the fairy tale and happily-ever-after. "Maybe your expectations were too high."

"And maybe you don't know anything about it," she snapped.

The flashes of anger in her eyes were so unlike her that he took heed of her warning to back off. "I guess I don't. Sorry if I stepped where I shouldn't have. Do you want to leave or do you want to stay?"

"I'd like to stay a little while longer."

He guessed the reason why. "Decided you have something to prove?"

"Yes," she answered quickly. "Pete Cantrell doesn't mean anything to me any more, and I'm not going to let him think he does by leaving."

"Making him a little jealous wouldn't hurt, either, I suppose," Zack drawled, disliking the idea she was using him.

Her anger flared even brighter and she stood. "I wouldn't do that to you and if you think I would, then we *shouldn't* stay."

Simply staring at her for a few moments, he finally stood, too. "I like this one. How about teaching me the two-step."

There was so much about Lucy that he was attracted to. As the anger disappeared from her eyes, and she gave him a small smile, he felt that attraction grow even stronger.

"The two-step it is," she said with a nod toward the dance floor.

He took her arm and decided Pete Cantrell was a total fool.

Although Lucy danced with Zack again, they weren't as easy with each other and they didn't dance quite as close. She was both relieved and disappointed. Seeing Pete Cantrell had brought back sad memories. She had no feelings for him any more, not even the resentment that had lingered for a while. But she remembered all too well why he'd walked away. She couldn't have children. Not ever. Men wanted children. Heirs somehow made them feel immortal. Maybe she should have told Zack. But why should she when he wasn't going to stay? Still the reminder that she wasn't a whole woman put her reserve up again. It wasn't only her reserve that made dancing different. Zack was different. Meeting Pete Cantrell had changed something in his eyes and she still didn't know him well enough to read that part of him. He was a complicated man and she wanted to know more about his past. But he obviously didn't want to tell her any more than she wanted to tell him about her failure with Pete Cantrell. Although he'd confided in her about his wife and child, she thought he was still holding something back and she wondered why. What were the secrets he kept, and why was he afraid to share them?

An hour later, the wind whipped against the car as they drove back to the Rising Star. Winter was setting in and Lucy wished Zack would at least stay until Christmas. He switched on the radio and they listened to soft, sentimental music that brought back memories of Pete, but only for an instant. They were overtaken by memories of Zack, kissing her and holding her in his arms while they danced.

As they pulled onto the road leading to the house, Zack asked, "Want me to drop you off?"

"No, I'll ride over to the garage with you."

At the old wooden outbuilding, he got out and opened the door, then climbed back in and drove the car into the garage, letting it idle for a few moments.

When he switched it off, they could hear the sound of the wind against the clapboard and neither of them moved.

Zack's voice was husky in the darkness. "I had a good time tonight."

She had, too, in spite of running into Pete. "I'm glad. Maybe if you stay long enough we can do it again." She heard the unsnapping of his seatbelt and could just make him out in the shadows as he turned to face her.

"Did you ever sleep with Pete Cantrell?"

"Zack!"

"You can tell me it's none of my business, but I still want to know. Did you?"

She thought she heard an almost proprietary note in his voice, but that wasn't possible, was it? There was really no reason to pretend she was more experienced than she was. "No, I didn't. Pete's very old-fashioned and so am I."

"Sometimes people use that excuse when the spark's not there."

"Maybe. But I don't intend to sleep with a man until I'm committed to him and he's committed to me. There's more to it than just being old-fashioned."

He leaned toward her then and slid his hand under her hair. "There's fire between us, Lucy, and the question is, do we want to get burnt by it?"

He bent his head and kissed her.

The kiss was more possessive and fiercely passionate than she expected. She thought about resisting and moving away. She thought about how she felt…and about commitment. But Zack's lips and the seductive stroke of his tongue scattered her thoughts until she forgot time and place and what she should or shouldn't do. She strained toward him over the arm rest and suddenly he shoved it upright to bring her closer, to meld their mouths more seriously, to delve deeper. Cold seeped into the car, but all she could feel was the heat between them and the longing to take and give more. She laced her hands in his thick hair and held onto him wanting to remember everything about the moment…yearning to know everything about him. But if she found out everything about him, she'd have to tell him everything about her. Since Pete had walked out on her, she'd felt as if she were less than a woman, unable to give a man what he wanted or needed. Wouldn't Zack see her the same way? She couldn't bear that. She couldn't bear seeing pity rather than desire. And if they kept this up, they *were* going to get burned. Badly.

Although pushing away was the last thing in the world she wanted to do, she did it anyway.

"Too much fire for an old-fashioned girl?" he asked.

"Too much fire when I know you'll be leaving before I even get to know you."

The silence became as cold as the weather outside.

"We'd better go in."

Zack opened his car door and she opened hers, wishing he wanted roots and a future. Yet knowing even if he did, she might not be able to provide it.

Chapter Seven

When Zack stepped through the airplane hangar door into the arena, he stopped and watched. Marty was on horseback holding back a few head of cattle as Lucy worked one of the horses. Zack could see she was an expert at what she did. She moved with the horse as if they were one, cutting one steer from the rest.

He hadn't spoken to her since they'd come in from the car last night, his body still singing from what they'd done there. While he'd gone to his room, she'd climbed the stairs, with a murmured good night. This morning, she'd either skipped breakfast or eaten later. He wished she weren't so old-fashioned...or downright scared. He wished she could forget about commitment and just think about pleasure.

But then she wouldn't be Lucy.

"She's something to watch, isn't she?" Rick had come in and was now standing beside him. Zack hadn't noticed because he was focused on Lucy.

"She sure is. I imagine she's been riding since she could walk."

Her older brother chuckled. "Practically. Even when she was a little thing she had no fear of horses. Just wanted to sit on top of one. And even after her accident…" Rick stopped abruptly.

"What accident?" Zack asked.

"She hasn't told you?"

Zack shook his head.

"When she was seventeen, she took a pretty bad spill and landed in the hospital."

"She's tough. I could see she wouldn't let an accident interfere with what she wanted to do."

"She's strong, Zack, but maybe not quite as strong as she seems." There was a warning in Rick's voice.

Shifting his stance, Zack unzipped his coat. "How long did she date Pete Cantrell?"

Rick looked surprised Zack knew about that, but he answered, "A few months."

"Did *she* break it off, or did he?" Zack wanted to know.

"You'd better ask her what happened if you think you have the right to know."

Zack wasn't sure if he had the right, but he sure wanted it. "You all think you have to protect Lucy."

With a shrug, Rick responded, "That's what families do. I've watched her skin her knees climbing trees, talk to horses as if they were people, work as hard as me or Marty beside Dad. So when she had that accident, we all sat by her bed and prayed she'd be okay again. How could I not want to protect her?"

"Tell me this. Did Cantrell hurt her?"

The word was slow in coming, but finally Rick answered. "Yes. And I don't want to see her get hurt like that again."

"Meaning that I should stay away from her?"

"Meaning just be aware of every step you take with her. You're a drifter, Zack. She's not. Never will be. She's tied to the Rising Star and us and doesn't want it any differently."

Lucy stopped working, brought her horse to the edge of the arena and dismounted. "After lunch, we'll bring in some fresh cattle," she called to Marty.

This was the first time Zack had seen her younger brother cooperating and working.

When Lucy came over to him, Rick went to help Marty.

"Have you been up to the house yet?" she asked, looking concerned.

"No, why?"

"Mom had a sore throat this morning. I think she caught Josh's cold. I told her we'd just grab sandwiches for lunch."

"Why don't we go check on her," he suggested, wanting to put his arm around Lucy, wanting to draw her into his arms again. Instead he fell into step beside her as they left the arena and walked toward the house. Cold air whipped around them, blowing Lucy's hair across her cheek.

Unable to help himself, Zack stretched out his hand and lifted the hood of her jacket onto her head. "Button up," he ordered.

She gave him a quick look. "I'm used to cold weather, Zack. I just haven't gotten out my earmuffs yet."

Stopping, he faced her, found the strings to her hood at her neck and pulled them so her hood would stay on her head. Then he tied a bow under her chin. His fingers brushed her skin and the stirrings of desire that had begun when he'd watched her in the arena became stronger. Her eyes mirrored her awareness of him. It was an awareness he wished he could take advantage of and respond to. But there were so many warnings in his head, not just from Rick but from himself that he turned away from her and started toward the house again.

At the stoop, Zack let Lucy precede him inside. Esther was at the range and the kitchen smelled as it always did at meal time, welcoming and homey.

Seeing the pot of soup on the stove and the fresh baked bread on the counter, Lucy scolded her mother. "I told you sandwiches would be fine. How are you feeling?"

Lucy went up to her mother and touched her cheek. "You're warm."

"Of course I'm warm. I've been standing in front of the stove."

"Mrs. McIntyre, it wouldn't hurt to rest a little bit."

"So you're in on this, too?" she asked, chagrined.

Zack smiled at her, using his best bedside charm. "I see how hard you work and if you're feeling a bit under the weather, there's no reason not to pamper yourself a little, is there? If you want to rest after lunch, Lucy and I can clean up."

Lucy's approving smile at his words made his heart beat faster.

"You know we can, Mom. And I can make supper. Take off for the afternoon and rest. You can catch up on reading or crocheting or watch TV."

"Lucy McIntyre, you know I don't watch TV much. I have too many other things to do. With Thanksgiving and Christmas coming—"

Lucy rolled her eyes. "So start writing the family letter and take a nap when you get tired."

Her mother finally gave in. "I would be getting something done that way. Are you sure you have time to make supper?"

"Sure do. Marty was helping me this morning and I'm sure if I ask, he'll help this afternoon."

Esther nodded her head approvingly. "I think he's finally coming around."

Zack hoped Esther McIntyre was right about her son, but he had his doubts.

Lunch went smoothly. Rick had gone home to eat with Mary Jo. Marty was quiet but Zack didn't feel the hostility that had been there before. Maybe he was coming to terms with whatever his problems were.

After Lucy urged her mother to go up to her bedroom to rest, Marty and Tom went out to the barn, but Zack stayed behind with Lucy.

"I don't need your help," she told him.

"If you want to get back to work, two of us getting it done will go a lot faster."

"All right. Why don't you load the dishwasher while I wash up the pots and baking pans? Mom doesn't like to put them in."

They worked together companionably, Zack filling

the dishwasher, Lucy filling the sink with hot water and soap suds. He finished before she did and reached around her to pick up a towel to dry the pots she'd set in the drainer. His arms surrounded her and he could feel her pull in her breath and hold it.

"You always smell so good," he breathed close to her ear.

"I probably smell like horses," she said on a long breath.

He shook his head. "Never."

Leaning away from her then, he stood beside her and picked up the soup pot to dry. When she transferred a baking pan from the sink to the rack, suds from the back of her hand floated onto Zack's wrist. His gaze met hers. Slipping his fingers under the little puffs of suds, he tapped her nose with them. She smiled, swiped at her nose then playfully picked up a handful and blew them at him.

Suddenly they both went still and just gazed into each other's eyes. Zack suspected she was remembering the night before as was he.

Placing the towel on the counter, he reached toward her and ran his thumb over her cheekbone. "Maybe I should leave now."

She shook her head. "I don't want you to. Besides, Dad and Rick need your help."

"If I stay, we're headed for trouble."

"If you stay, it might be something *other* than trouble."

"Oh, Lucy, I don't have dreams left. You do. Don't you see how different we are?"

"I see the differences. But I see other things, too."

"You mean *feel* other things, don't you?" he asked huskily.

With her imperceptible nod, he couldn't help but draw her toward him. He couldn't help but lower his head to hers. He couldn't help but kiss her long and slow and deep.

They were locked in each other's arms when the kitchen door opened. Zack broke away from her and raised his head to see Rick standing there watching them.

Lucy's blush told the story.

"Sorry," Rick said, not looking sorry at all. "Dad wants to know if you can mend fence this afternoon while I exercise some of the mares."

"No problem," Zack said, not intimidated by Rick's arched brows and the questions in his eyes.

"Go ahead, Zack," Lucy said. "I'll finish these."

It was a strange feeling. Zack didn't want to leave her. But that was ridiculous. Even in his marriage he and his wife had gone their separate ways every morning. He'd never felt this yearning ache that made him want to stay.

But more than anything else, that yearning ache had him folding the towel and setting it on the counter. Then he strode across the kitchen, plucked his coat from the hook and shrugged into it. Setting his hat on his head, he didn't look back at Lucy and followed Rick outside.

He wasn't sure what he expected from Rick, but all he got was a direct look and the warning, "Remember what I said earlier, Zack."

They headed toward the barn and Rick's warning filled his mind again, but his body was still humming from the effects of Lucy's kiss. He knew he soon had to decide whether desire was more important than good sense.

When Esther invited Zack to go along to church with them on Sunday morning and he declined, Lucy had the feeling that he'd never really faced the loss of his wife and child. She knew sometime it was going to hit him and hit him hard. He ate Sunday dinner with them, though, and then spent the afternoon playing chess with her father. There had been people bustling about all day and Lucy hadn't had a minute alone with him. Maybe that was just as well.

Before she turned in for the night, she stopped at her mother's room. Her mom had felt better today, but she'd decided to go to bed early.

Lucy rapped gently on the door.

"Come in," her mother called.

Lucy stepped inside. Her mother had a comfortable, old robe belted around her and she was sitting in the rocker, reading by the floor lamp. A colorful quilt was tucked over her lap.

"How are you feeling, Mom?"

"Still a little tired. But I'll be set by Thursday if that's what you're worrying about."

Thursday was Thanksgiving. "I'm not worried. You know Mary Jo and I can handle the meal if we have to."

"Well, you won't have to. I'll be baking my pumpkin pies on Wednesday just like always."

Lucy crossed to the bed and sat on the corner of the four-poster. "Did you date anyone before Dad?" she asked, glad her father had gone out to the barns with Zack for that last evening check.

Esther looked surprised. "That depends on what you mean by dating. I went to the movies now and then with some fellas, but it wasn't until your dad came along that I wanted to be with someone every spare moment I could. That's how I knew he was the one."

"So you knew from the beginning?"

"Almost from the first moment he smiled at me." Esther set her book on her lap. "What's worrying you, honey? Is it Zack?"

"I feel things with him I never felt before...things that are making me wonder how I should act and what I should do."

"Sometimes it's hard to see right and wrong when you fall in love. Sometimes there is no right and wrong. But I always believed I shouldn't get serious about a man or get too close to a man unless we were thinking about marriage."

"Zack's not even ready to stay in one place," Lucy admitted.

"He's staying here, isn't he?"

"That's only temporary."

"What do you want, Lucy?" Her mother's eyes were kind and not the least bit judgmental.

"I want to feel what I'm feeling. I don't want to be afraid of it. I want to explore whatever this is with Zack."

"But—" her mother prompted.

"But I don't know if that's right to do, and I don't know how much I'll get hurt by doing it."

"There's always a chance you'll get hurt when you love someone, whether it's a brother or a sister or a friend or a man. But that doesn't mean you shouldn't love. It also doesn't mean you should act recklessly."

She was not reckless whenever she was with Zack. That was the problem. But she also knew her values would rein in any impulse. At least she'd known that until now.

"Finding happiness, Lucy, doesn't come in a leap. It comes in small steps," her mother offered. "You don't know Zack very well yet. Maybe you need a few more smaller steps before you can decide what you *should* do."

Standing, Lucy went over to her mother, bent down and kissed her cheek. "Thanks, Mom."

Esther gave her a hug. "Anytime."

When Lucy left her mother's room, she thought about the picture in her dresser drawer. Going to her bedroom, she crossed to the dresser and opened the drawer, taking out the photo.

Small steps, her mother had said. That didn't mean only with Zack. She'd thought about showing the picture to her mother, but she couldn't bear hurting her in any way.

She studied the two babies in the picture. But she *did* want to know if she had a sister. Tomorrow morning she'd call John Buckley and tell him to make inquiries. Nothing might come of it so she didn't want to cause a commotion unnecessarily. If and when he had information for her, then she'd talk to her parents.

And in the meantime?

She'd remember to take very small steps with Zack.

Preparations for Thanksgiving began early Wednesday. Lucy and Mary Jo helped her mother bake pies, bread, and generally get ready for the next day. When Josh got home from school, he wanted to join in, too.

Zack walked into the commotion late Wednesday afternoon.

Josh ran over to him. "Are you going to help for Thanksgiving?"

"Thanksgiving," Zack said thoughtfully. "I guess it is that time of year." Looking down at the little boy, he asked, "And just what kind of help do you need?"

Mary Jo said, "Josh, Zack's been working all day. Let him get a rest before you give him more work."

Zack chuckled. "I don't need a rest, but I sure could use a shower. After that, Josh, you could show me what we need to do. Okay?"

In less than twenty minutes, Zack had returned to the kitchen. Lucy pointed to the two loaves of bread sitting on the table and the large pans beside it. "You and Josh could pull the bread for the filling. How about that? Josh knows how we do it. He can show you."

As Lucy helped her mother prepare vegetables for dinner, she was aware that Zack was quieter than usual. He helped Josh finish with the bread and then they all sat down to the meal. But he didn't enter any of the conversations and she suspected she knew why.

He wasn't around after they cleaned up dinner and Mary Jo mentioned that she'd seen him walking toward the barn. Slipping on her jacket, Lucy went outside.

The sky twinkled with at least a thousand stars as the wind brought the fragrance of pine. By the glow of the moon, she could see the tips of the mountains. There was no place else on earth she'd rather be.

The all-purpose barn was midway between Mary Jo and Rick's house and her parents'. Lucy spotted a light inside and walked toward it, taking her time enjoying the stillness of the night. When she opened the door, the scent of hay and the swish of a horse's tail greeted her. Peering down the walkway, she saw Zack at Blazer's stall, one boot propped on the bottom rung, his elbows resting on the top rung, his Stetson low on his forehead. As she walked toward him, her heart pumped faster. She stopped when she reached him, then turned and offered Blazer her hand.

"Communing with him?" she asked.

"Are you talking to me or Blazer?"

Though the question was meant to be teasing, there was no amusement in Zack's voice. "Both of you, I suppose."

As Blazer let her pet his nose, Zack asked, "How's he doing?"

"Much better. He hardly shies away from me at all now. It's time to get him used to some others. If you'd like to ride him, we could have a practice session soon."

He gave her a speculative look. "Why me? Don't you think Rick might do a better job?"

"He's not this quiet around Rick."

Zack straightened. "I could try it, I guess."

They stood there together in silence as she continued to stroke Blazer's nose. Finally she brought up the subject that had brought her to the barn. "I imagine the holidays are painful for you."

"I tried to forget Thanksgiving was this week."

"But that didn't work?" she prompted.

"Lucy, I don't want to talk about it."

"That's probably why you couldn't forget it."

He faced her, exasperation evident. "You're something, you know that? One minute I think you're shy and vulnerable, the next you're determined as all get out. You want me to look at things I'd rather forget. Yet you want to find your sister but are afraid to do it. Maybe you need to turn some of that determination into your own life."

She'd thought she could help him. She'd thought she could listen. But if he was going to try and hurt her because he hurt, it was better not to be here. Giving Blazer a last pat, she turned away and started down the walkway.

But Zack caught up to her and clasped her arm. "Lucy, wait."

"I'm not going to pry, Zack, if you don't want me to. And for your information, I called John Buckley. He's going to start looking for my sister."

Even in the dim light of the barn, she could see the surprise on his face. "What made you decide?"

"The holidays, I guess. And something you said. What if my sister needs me more than I need her."

Zack stood there silently for a few moments, his

hand still on her arm. Finally he released it. "You're right. I don't like thinking about holidays I had on my family's ranch when I was a kid. Those were happy times. But my dad lost the ranch when times were tough. I was a teenager then. He'd stopped smoking years before, but after we had to move from the ranch, he took it up again. And he died of lung cancer the summer after I graduated from high school." Zack slipped the pen knife from his pocket and studied it. "He gave me this when he was diagnosed."

"Oh, Zack, I'm sorry. What about your mom?"

"She died of a broken heart. She loved him so much I don't think she wanted to go on without him. I had earned a scholarship to college and she encouraged me to go because she said my father would have wanted that. I knew she was lonely. I knew she missed Dad and I called as often as I could. But her heart developed an arrhythmia—an irregularity that she didn't tell me about. She died one night in her sleep."

Lucy absolutely didn't know what to say. Zack had lost so many people dear to him, what *could* she say?

"So, no, I don't like to think about those holidays with my parents or the ones I had with my wife, or the future ones we might have had with a child. I realized tonight that on the road, I could pretty much forget about them. Here I can't."

"Holidays are meant to be enjoyed, Zack, even when we've lost somebody we love."

"And just who have you lost?" he demanded. "You've got a family, a large one, who loves you and wants to protect you."

"You're right. I haven't lost anyone I love. I lost Pete, but now I'm not sure how much I did actually love him. When the holidays came around after we broke up, I didn't miss him. It was more—" She stopped abruptly and didn't finish the thought. "But I have lost, Zack. I lost my parents—my biological parents. That fact is there under the surface every day. And I've lost other things. That doesn't mean I shouldn't experience joy anymore, or feel happy, or reach out and grab whatever happiness can come my way. Don't you think your parents as well as your wife would want you to put your life back together?"

"What makes you think my life isn't together?"

She knew he wasn't blind. He was just frustratingly stubborn. "Tell me something, Zack. Do you want to still be riding around on a Harley when your hair turns grey? Do you want to spend each year trying to skip holidays? Do you want to be alone for the rest of your life?"

His stance grew defensive, his back straight and rigid. "It shouldn't matter to you what I want because my life isn't any of your concern."

She knew the angry sparks in his eyes masked a world of pain, but she didn't stop him when he strode by her. She just watched him walk out into the cold night...alone.

Lucy didn't see Zack again until the next morning when she and her mom were sliding the turkey into the oven. He passed through the kitchen on his way outside, nodded, and gave them a polite good morning. But that was all. Lucy hardly returned the greeting before he was out on the porch.

"You two have a fight?" Esther asked.

"I'm not sure what we had. He won't look at his pain, Mom, so it's never going to go away."

"Child, a man doesn't want to feel weak, and pain makes him feel weak. You showing it to him is just going to make him angry."

Lucy's eyes filled with tears and she wasn't even sure why.

Esther patted her arm. "Without meaning to, we're rubbing everything he doesn't have in his face."

"But he *could* have it."

"He just needs some time to get used to the idea. Don't push him, Lucy. He'll only put more distance between you."

Her mother was usually right and all she could do was wait for Zack to heal…or leave.

As the McIntyre clan gathered before dinner, Zack stretched on the floor beside Josh building a house. He'd tried to numb himself against everything going on around him. He'd even thought about driving into town today. Staying away. Letting the family celebrate together. But when he came back, he'd have to face Lucy. The more courageous thing was to stay and just try to endure anything that came up.

As Tom placed the turkey in the middle of the table, Esther gave them all a place to sit. Like the night he'd arrived, he sat with Lucy on his left and Josh on his right. Tom sat at the head of the table and smiled at them all. "Before I carve the turkey, we must say grace on this wonderful day. Let's all take hands."

Before Zack could even think about what Tom had said, Josh grabbed his hand. On his other side, Lucy glanced at him and he knew he couldn't keep himself apart right now. He covered her hand with his and waited.

Tom said, "Dear Lord. We thank you for every person around our table and for all the goodness you've given us this year. We have a wonderful way of life and we appreciate every bit of it. We also want to particularly thank you for sending us a man who has been a helper and friend. We thank you for Zackary Burke, his kindness and hard work."

Zack felt his chest tighten and his throat constrict. Tom's words hurt him and he wasn't sure why. This family had made him a part of their lives and he was the one who should be thanking *them*. But instead, he'd kept his heart hard. If he'd skipped out today, they would have been hurt and he would have missed feeling part of something bigger than himself.

He didn't hear the rest of what Tom said and when he glanced at Lucy, she had her head bowed. But as if feeling his gaze, she turned toward him. When Tom had finished and the McIntyres began passing food, Zack squeezed her hand.

Some of the sadness he'd felt for so long lifted during the meal as he became involved in more than one conversation and ate more food than he could ever remember eating at one sitting. Even Marty was making an effort to be amiable and Zack took it at face value.

After pumpkin pie with whipped cream and two

cups of coffee, Zack smiled at Lucy. "I think I need a very long walk."

"Do you want company?" she asked.

Suddenly he did. He wanted *her* company. "Sure."

Everyone helped clean up and after the last pan was washed and dried, Lucy put on her jacket and joined him on the porch. The sky had become grey and the air damp with winter. They started walking down the lane that led to the main road.

They walked for a stretch without talking and then he said, "Your family is something to treasure, Lucy. You're very lucky."

"I know."

They continued walking. As she breathed, her breath puffed white into the air. He moved a little closer to her. "I planned to put down roots again with my wife…roots like I'd had with my parents on the ranch. But we didn't have the chance."

"Does that mean you want them?" Lucy asked hopefully.

"Roots and the pain of losing seem to go together right now."

"Maybe that will change."

Snow began falling then, lightly, settling on their hair and coats. Lucy smiled and held her hand out to catch the flakes. "Our first snow."

Zack didn't know what the future would bring, but for right now, he just wanted to enjoy being with Lucy. Draping his arm around her shoulders, he pulled her close for a moment. "We'd better go back to the house. You forgot your earmuffs again."

Laughing, she stared up at him. He couldn't resist the allure of her lips and he bent and kissed her as snow flurried softly around them.

When they broke apart, he sent up his own prayer of thanks—for Thanksgiving and the McIntyres. But especially for Lucy.

Chapter Eight

The Friday after Thanksgiving on the Rising Star was business as usual. Preparations for winter included repairs on all the outbuildings as well as the normal chores. Zack hardly had a chance to speak to Lucy all day. He even lost track of her after supper as he helped Tom clean out a few stalls in the mares' barn. Finally he went looking for her.

The fine coating of snow that had fallen yesterday had melted in the sun. When he saw lights on in the all-purpose barn, he headed that way. Even before he opened the door he heard a commotion inside, a loud neigh, a striking of hooves. What the blazes was going on?

As he threw open the door and rushed inside, he heard Marty shout, then curse.

"Marty, wait," Lucy yelled above the furor. "Don't scare him like that." Marty had picked up a broom and was holding it across himself like a protective shield.

Before Zack could get to the stall, Lucy had slipped inside between Marty and the horse. Blazer reared up again and Zack was terrified that the horse's hooves would slash at her, or worse yet, knock her down under him. But he knew if he yelled, he might only make the situation worse.

"Whoa, boy. Easy now," she crooned to him, despite the horse's obvious agitation.

When Blazer reared up again, his hoof glanced her shoulder, knocking her against the stall door.

Rushing toward her, Zack ran inside and pushed Marty out of the way. "Get out of here," he said between clenched teeth as he moved toward the horse, determined to keep Blazer away so he wouldn't hurt Lucy again.

"Whoa, boy," he said in a loud, firm voice. "Whoa! It's okay. No one's going to hurt you. Take it easy now." The horse's head swung toward Zack as he kept talking, then finally patted the horse's neck.

"Lucy, move out," he said quietly but firmly.

She was holding her shoulder. "I'm all right."

"Move out," Zack said again, and this time she did as he ordered.

He ran his hand down the horse's neck, patting, talking, calming. It wasn't the way Lucy did it, but it worked. Blazer snorted softly, pawed at the ground, but didn't rear up again.

Finally Zack moved out of the stall, shut the door and glared at Marty. "What the hell were you doing to him?"

"Not a damn thing. I just wanted him out of there so I could clean up. He wouldn't come."

"So you what—you took the broom to him?" Zack's restrained fury was easy to hear.

"I just tried to shoo him—"

"You've been around horses all of your life! You should know better. You put Lucy in danger. She could have been killed in there."

Marty's cheeks flushed and he threw the broom to the ground. "You think you know so much about it? *You* take care of him from now on. You clean out his stall." Without a backward glance, he walked out of the barn and left Zack there with Lucy.

"And you." Zack said with almost as much anger as he gestured to her. "You should have known better than to go inside there. What were you thinking?"

"I didn't want Blazer to hurt himself or Marty. *That's* what I was thinking."

When he saw she wasn't about to back down or admit *she'd* been wrong, he shook his head. "Let me look at your shoulder. Take off your jacket."

"I'm fine, Zack."

"Take off your jacket," he said evenly.

Unzipping her coat, she shrugged out of it, but she winced as she pulled it over her left arm.

She was wearing a soft cotton blouse. Her collar was open at the neck and he could see her pulse beating there. But he ignored the inclination to touch her in a more than professional way. When he felt the shoulder joint, that pressure didn't seem to cause her pain.

"Raise your arm," he said matter-of-factly.

She lifted it without any trouble, but when she brought it back down again, she winced.

"I think it's just bruised. If you put ice on it that should help." Then he added, "I've had enough spills from horses and from my motorcycle to know what works and what doesn't."

She was gazing up at him with wide eyes. "Thank you, Zack."

"For what?" he asked gruffly.

"For protecting me. For calming Blazer. I just couldn't bear to see him so afraid."

Zack's anger vanished and as it did, he realized it was fear that had fueled it. He couldn't bear the thought of something happening to Lucy.

Wrapping his arms around her, he pulled her close to him. The beats of their hearts synchronized. Leaning away slightly, he cupped her chin then kissed her. It started out easy and tender, but soon blazed high and wild. The kiss became much more than a blending of lips and a teasing of tongues as their bodies strained toward each other. He'd worn an insulated vest instead of a coat to give himself freedom of movement. It was an unwelcome barrier between them.

Raising his head, he shrugged the vest off and then brought her to him again. But this time he reached between them and when his hand covered her breast, she moaned.

"Lucy, I want you," he murmured, kissing her neck, then her ear, then her temple.

"I want you, too," she whispered.

He reined in his desire. "But you're hurt. You need ice on your shoulder and—"

"The ice can wait," she insisted as she stroked his jaw and looked deep into his eyes. "Mom and Dad are at the house. Marty surely is not going to come back in."

He kissed her again and then again after that, almost unable to believe what she was suggesting. "But you said you need commitment. You said—"

She stopped him again by putting her fingers over his lips. "I've never felt before what I'm feeling with you, and maybe it's time to stop thinking about it and just feel it."

He pressed his palm against her breast and when she sighed against his lips, he wanted to give her more pleasure than she could ever imagine. Backing her into an empty stall, he took her down with him until they were on their knees, kissing each other, touching, demanding more. His hands went to the buttons on her blouse and hers to his shirt. Carefully he helped take her blouse off, then he unhooked her bra. She tugged on his shirt till he ridded himself of it. When he then took her against him, felt her breasts against his chest and breathed in the smell of lilacs, he became dizzy with it. Their kisses became more fervent, their touching more frenzied. Stretching out on the hay, so careful of her shoulder, he gathered her on top of him, kissing her the whole time, feeling her against him, wanting satisfaction so badly he could taste it.

She whispered in his ear, "Zack, tell me what to do."

"You don't have to do anything," he said, touching her breasts, watching the desire flare higher in her eyes. "We already have the magic, Lucy. That's what matters."

When he kissed her this time, his hands cupped her buttocks and pressed her against him. As she moved sensuously in his arms, he groaned from the pleasure of it. When their bodies joined, they'd be perfect together. He knew it.

A warning bell went off in his mind and he couldn't figure out why, so caught up was he in the passion engulfing them both. But the warning grew louder and he was forced to think…think…

All at once he realized why the warning bell had sounded, and he reluctantly broke their kiss. "Lucy."

"What?" she murmured, gazing into his eyes.

"We can't do this. I don't have any protection."

She went very still and he felt an intake of breath before she said, "We don't need protection."

"Why not?" He suddenly hoped she was taking birth control pills to regulate her period or something as simple as that.

"Because I'm sterile."

Her voice shook on the word and he was stunned. "How?"

"Why does it matter? Why can't we just—"

"Lucy," he chastised gently. "Tell me."

Before he could stop her, she scrambled away from him and sat in the hay. "I was in a riding accident when I was seventeen. I broke my pelvis and my ovaries were damaged. There is no doubt, Zack. I can't have children." She was looking at him strangely and he didn't know what to say, except…

"I'm sorry."

"So am I," she said sadly.

He wasn't sure what to do next. He felt he needed to give her revelation the respect it deserved and taking up where they had left off just didn't seem respectful.

Rising to his knees, he looked down on her. "It's not fair. You'd make a wonderful mother."

"I don't want your pity, Zack. I can have a full life without having babies."

There was a defensiveness about her, and he didn't know where it was coming from.

"Sympathy isn't pity."

She carefully shrugged into her bra and blouse and rose to her feet. "It's close."

Before she put on her blouse, he saw the bruise starting to color on her shoulder. It was probably better nothing had happened. She needed an ice pack and he needed…to think.

Slipping on his shirt, he buttoned it and tucked it into his jeans.

Lucy was already outside of the stall checking on Blazer whose stall hadn't been cleaned.

"Go on up to the house and take care of your shoulder. I'll clean out his stall."

For once, she didn't argue with him. Avoiding his gaze, she slung her jacket over her arm, walked between the stalls and out the barn door.

Zack felt as if he'd done something terribly wrong and he didn't know what that was.

Tears flowed down Lucy's cheeks as she walked to the house. Zack's desire had vanished as fast as Pete's. She'd seen the change in his eyes.

After she swiped at her tears, she carefully pulled

on her jacket and found a tissue in the pocket. Blowing her nose, she let the cold air dry the rest of her tears and ruffle her hair. By the time she went inside, she had to be composed. If she could just make it to her room…

But as she neared the porch, she saw Marty standing there under the glow of the porch light. He came down to meet her.

"Lucy, I'm sorry. I never want anything to hurt you. You know that, don't you?"

She was close enough to him that she could smell liquor on his breath. "Have you been drinking?"

"A shot. That's all. Honest."

"Why even one?"

"Because I felt like a fool. I didn't know how to face you."

"But you *are* facing me and, Marty, I don't want you to ever think you need to take a drink to do that." She saw the dejection in his eyes…the real sorrow that she might have been hurt.

Ignoring the soreness in her shoulder, she wrapped her arms around him and held him tight. "Maybe Zack's right. You do need help."

He pulled away. "I don't need help. I'm fine."

Marty might still be in denial, but she wasn't. Yet she also knew he wouldn't accept help until he could admit he needed it. "If you don't have the patience for Blazer, just stay away from him, okay?"

"Okay," he said. "How's your arm?"

"I need to put ice on it. But that's going to make me cold. So why don't you fix hot chocolate and we'll have it together before we go upstairs."

"Sounds good to me."

Hooking her good arm through his, they climbed the steps together and Lucy hoped tonight hadn't been a total fiasco. Maybe what had happened with Blazer and to her would make Marty see more clearly. Only time would tell.

And only time would tell if Zack's attitude toward her had changed…if the magic between them had gone up in smoke because she wasn't a whole woman.

On Saturday morning, Lucy remained in her room until she knew Zack would be dressed, finished with breakfast, and out of the house. She didn't want to see more pity in his eyes.

By the time she went downstairs, everyone was gone, even her mother. There was a note on the kitchen table from her mom telling Lucy she had gone up to Mary Jo's to spend the morning with Josh while Mary Jo shopped. Everyone was on their own for lunch but she'd be back midafternoon.

Lucy was setting the teapot on the stove to boil when her cell phone rang. Taking it from her pocket, she answered the call. "Hello?"

"Lucy? It's John Buckley. Do you have a minute?"

Her heart pounding, she crossed to the living room and sat on the sofa. "Yes, I do."

"I have some news for you. Good news and bad."

"Give me the good news first."

"I searched birth records in Cheyenne, Cody and

Laramie for the date you were born. You and your sister were born to Jeanette Sullivan in Laramie."

Lucy could hardly breathe. "What else did you find?"

"Not much. There was a note that one baby was given up for adoption, the other wasn't."

This news was like a sudden ten-ton weight. "That means my mother kept my sister…but not me."

"I assume that's so. I can't find anything to contradict that."

She sucked in a large breath of air. "Did you find out where they are?"

The lawyer's voice became even kinder if that was possible. "This is the bad news."

Lucy fortified herself the best she could.

"A Jeanette Sullivan died in Laramie two years after you were born. I couldn't find a trail for your sister. Twenty years ago record-keeping wasn't what it is today."

No trail. That didn't mean she was dead…like her birth mother. Lucy felt emotion welling up in her eyes and blinked fast. "Do you know my sister's name?"

"I don't, Lucy. That's another reason I can't find a lead. You came to Esther and Tom without a name. *They* named you. On the birth records, you were listed as Baby Girl Sullivan #1 and your sister was Baby Girl Sullivan #2. So I suppose even though your mother took your sister home with her, she didn't name her right away. Records weren't computerized then the way they are now," he reminded her again.

"So we can't find her?"

He sighed. "I can check every woman around your age with the last name of Sullivan in Laramie and Cody and everywhere in between. But it could take forever. And what if she married? What if she moved out of the state? I think this is beyond my scope and skills. If you want to pursue this, you should really think about hiring a private investigator."

"Don't they charge a lot? I'm not sure I could afford that. I do have some money saved—" Her parents paid her a salary and, for the most part, she stowed that in a retirement account. She could take a loan against that…

"They charge a daily fee and expenses."

She was quiet.

"You don't have to make a decision immediately. Think about it, Lucy. Just think about it. Maybe talk to your parents."

She did have so much to think about. "Okay, Mr. Buckley. I'll think about it and get back to you."

Lucy went through the day as if it were an ordinary one, but her mind was fashioning all kinds of scenarios around the information John Buckley had given her. Hiring a private investigator would be a big step. Should she do it? Were there any reputable ones in the area? She might have to go as far away as Laramie.

She wasn't ready to tell her parents about this yet. The truth was she needed a sounding board. In the past that might have been Marty. But not now. She realized there was one other person she trusted—Zack.

That evening, she waited until everyone went to bed. Then she went back downstairs and knocked on the door to his room. "It's Lucy," she called softly.

"Just a minute," he called back and she wondered if he'd already been asleep.

She heard the rustle of clothes, a chair being moved. In her mind's eye, she wondered what Zack slept in. She couldn't imagine him in pajamas. To her chagrin, she could easily imagine him in the nude!

When he came to the door, he was wearing a pair of sweat pants that hung low. Their drawstring fell just under his navel. Quickly she hiked her gaze up to his face. "Can we talk?"

"About what happened in the barn?"

Was he still thinking about it, too? "No, not about that. Mr. Buckley called me."

He caught the lowering of her voice. "Do you want to come in? Or do you want to sit in the living room?"

She didn't want to talk anywhere someone could overhear. "I'll come in," she decided as if she entered a man's bedroom every day. Feeling nervous, she slipped into the room, past Zack's bare chest. She reminded herself why she was there and crossed to the ladder-back chair and perched on it.

Zack sat on the bed across from her. "What did he tell you?"

After a look into Zack's eyes, the sparse way his room was decorated and the few things of his lying around, she said, "If you don't want to get involved in this, I understand. It's just…I need some advice."

He didn't say whether he did want to get involved or didn't. Rather he just asked, "About?"

She told him everything the lawyer had told her.

"What would you have done if he'd found your sister's name and address?" Zack asked.

That's one of the scenarios she'd tossed around in her head. "I would have gone to see her."

"So you do want to find her and you do want to meet her."

"Yes, I do."

Zack summed up her predicament. "Besides the fact that this seems impossible, the money outlay is troubling you."

"Yes. I'm concerned if my parents know I really want to do this, they'll offer to foot the bill. I can't let them do that."

Zack was quiet for a very long time.

"What are you thinking?"

"I'm thinking that maybe there was a reason I applied for this job."

She didn't understand. "A reason other than you looking for work? You aren't a P.I., are you?"

A guarded look filled his eyes but he answered, "No, I'm not." He stood and paced over to the window.

It was too dark to see anything out there. But she waited, knowing he was analyzing something in his mind.

"I'm not a private investigator but I know of one with a good reputation. He's friends with Linc Granger, the man I had that phone conversation with a couple of weeks ago."

"He's in California?"

"Yes, but Jake isn't the person I'd want you to talk to. His partner is."

"Why? Does he charge less?" she joked, though she really didn't feel like joking.

"No. His partner is a woman—Gillian Bradley. Her specialty and Jake's too now is finding missing persons, especially missing children. They have a foundation set up for it. People they help pay the usual fees if they can. But if they can't, the foundation covers it. Wealthier people they've helped or who have heard about the foundation fund their work."

"A not-for-profit P.I. firm?" That sounded like a contradiction of terms.

Zack studied her again, took another look out the window, then rubbed his hand down over his face.

"What *aren't* you telling me?"

He hesitated, then answered her. "I don't know how to say this. So I'll just say it. Gillian Bradley has a gift." She must have looked perplexed because he explained further. "My friend Linc and Gillian's husband Nathan are best friends. A few years ago, Nathan called Jake Donovan for help when his ex-wife disappeared with his daughters. Unfortunately, Jake met nothing but roadblocks and suggested Nathan look into Gillian's work. He did. She has a gift for finding people. She can tune into them—"

"Like a psychic?" Lucy asked astounded that someone as practical as Zack would be telling her this.

"She doesn't think of herself that way. She helped Linc, too. From what I understand, when Gillian was ten she was hit by lightning. After that, she had…sensations… feelings…could sense things others couldn't. It's quite possible she could help you."

"But she works with a P.I.?"

"Gillian and Jake work together. Jake does the investigative work if necessary, backing up or confirming what she finds out. They have a 99 percent success rate."

"Seriously?"

"Seriously."

"This is a lot to take in!"

"I know. But I've met Gillian and Jake. I heard how they helped Linc as well as Nathan. In addition I know Gillian found a little girl lost in the hills and Jake found a client's high school sweetheart. They're a team and could be just what you need. Besides, they'll help you and then you can donate whatever you can manage."

"You're sure about that?"

"I'm sure. It's a Karma thing. They help people and the funds just keep rolling in. It really is amazing."

"The foundation pays their salaries?"

"Yes. Approved by a board of directors. This is all above-board. They're good people, Lucy. I wouldn't recommend them if I didn't know for sure."

"How would this work? Would I have to go to California?"

"I'll have to call Linc to get in touch with Gillian. We'd have to see what her schedule is like. She and Nathan have a little boy and Nathan often has his girls from his first marriage staying with him. But it's possible she could fly in overnight. We'd have to see what she suggests."

"How does she work?"

"With pictures…personal belongings."

"I only have that one picture."

"I know. But it's worth a call, don't you think? I can call Linc right now and get Gillian's number if you want to do this."

Somehow she'd have to explain all of it to her parents and brothers—not just about having a sister but about consulting a psychic!

"Zack—"

He seemed to understand what she was thinking and feeling. Hunkering down beside her chair, he laid his hand on her arm and looked directly into her eyes. "You know about women's intuition. I'm sure you understand about a mom's intuition when looking after her child—a sixth sense, if you will, that can sometimes keep them out of harm's way."

"Or see into their heart," Lucy suggested.

"Exactly. Gillian's gift is much like a very strong intuition. Scientifically it boils down to that lightning strike scrambling her brain in such a way that she can now use a lot more of it than the average person. It's a talent…a gift…just like a prodigy might have the gift of music or numbers."

"And you believe in this gift?"

"In Linc's case, I heard about it working first-hand. And Nathan believes he never could have found his ex-wife and daughters without Gillian. You can talk to her. If you don't have a good feeling when you're finished, you can always look for a P.I. around here. But effective, honest ones can sometimes be hard to find."

"That's what Mr. Buckley said, too."

"Do you want to think about it?"

Lucy did think about it. She thought about her life at the Rising Star, about her brothers and parents, about Marty not willing to ask for help and the realization that she needed to. "I have thought about it. I'd like you to make the call."

Zack patted her hand, stood and went to the night stand for his phone. Then he dialed Linc's number.

Chapter Nine

Two days later, Gillian arrived at the Rising Star after Lucy and her dad had picked her up at the Long Brush regional airport. Already Lucy liked this woman who had brought her four-year-old son with her!

After Zack had called Linc Granger and then Gillian Bradley on Saturday morning, Lucy had faced her family at breakfast. She'd called Mary Jo and Rick asking them to join the family for pancakes. Then as Lucy's hands had gotten clammier, as her family had poured syrup and Zack had given her an encouraging nod, she'd cleared her throat and said, "I have something to tell all of you."

Every head had swung her way, even Josh's.

When her gaze had met Zack's, he'd looked concerned for her and asked, "Do you want me to leave?"

She shook her head. It was odd, but even after what had happened in the barn, she felt his support. She needed it now.

"What's the matter, honey?" her mom asked.

"A few weeks ago, John Buckley called me. He'd received some information about me when the lawyer died who'd handled my adoption. There was a picture with it of two identical babies. He suspected I might have a twin. Last week I asked him to start a search and he called me, giving me a few more details."

Her father looked astonished and said, "We knew your birth mother's name and that's about all."

"I know, Dad. And I always considered you and mom my real parents and didn't want to know more." Lucy could see her words touched her family.

Her mother asked, "Why didn't you tell us about this when John called?"

"I…didn't want to hurt you. I didn't want you to think you hadn't given me everything there was to give. I didn't want you to be disappointed that I was looking past what we have here."

"Oh, Lucy!" her mom exclaimed. "We'd never think that. Because of what we have here, we know how important ties are. A twin sister, honey. How wonderful! Does John know how to find her?"

Tears came to Lucy's eyes at her mother's words. Their had been no hesitation in them at all. So she'd told them everything John Buckley had told her.

Rick spoke for the first time. "So how are you going to find her? Do you want each of us to take a different town and make some calls?"

She was touched they'd do that for her. "I'm going to try another method first." Taking a deep breath, she shot ahead. "Zack's from California. He knows a P.I.

there who has a great success rate on missing person cases. He has a partner who…" Lucy had considered keeping the truth from her family and then decided against it. "She has a gift for finding missing persons."

"What kind of gift?" asked Marty who actually seemed to be listening.

"Some people would call her a psychic."

All of her family's surprised eyes were on her and Zack. She rushed on. "A foundation pays them to help anyone who can't pay. I have money saved and I would pay as much as I can."

"Sounds like a scam to me," Marty mumbled.

"Marty, hear your sister out," her dad advised.

And they had. Lucy had told them everything Zack had told her as well as additional background information Gillian had given her. After speaking with Gillian Bradley, Lucy had been convinced that she wanted to meet her and to enlist her help.

Marty had been against the idea, saying all psychics were frauds. Rick had said he was on the fence. Her parents were withholding their judgment until they met Gillian.

Now here Gillian Bradley was and Lucy was as nervous as she'd ever been. What if nothing came of this?

Then nothing would come of it.

Gillian wasn't at all what she'd expected. Maybe Lucy had expected a woman in new age flowing garb and swingy beaded earrings. Gillian Bradley wore jeans, boots, a down jacket and held the hand of her four-year-old son who she'd introduced as Matthew. Apparently her husband was away on a business trip and she hadn't wanted to leave her son with a babysitter. So Linc Granger had paid for a chartered jet and flown them here himself! Some friend Zack had.

Matthew was shy at first, but as soon as he saw Josh who was still home from school for the Thanksgiving holiday, he grinned. The two boys scampered off into the living room with Tom.

"So much for him needing to be with his mom," Gillian joked.

Lucy watched as Zack took Gillian's things to his room. He was going to sleep on the couch for the night. Matthew could bunk in a sleeping bag on the floor with him or with his mom.

Always wanting to help a stranger feel at home, Esther asked Gillian, "Can I get you anything?"

"No, I'm fine," Gillian assured her. "Linc made sure we had breakfast on the plane."

"This Linc person must be someone important," her mom commented.

Returning to the kitchen, Zack responded, "You probably watch some of his TV shows and the specials he produces. You might have even seen some of his films."

Zack wasn't telling them how he knew Linc but that was better left for another day. Lucy had enough to deal with for the moment.

Her mom must have seen that because she said, "I'll leave you alone now. If you need anything, just yell. I'll be in the living room helping to entertain the boys."

"What do we do first?" Lucy asked, glancing at Zack who was leaning against the counter.

Gillian motioned to the table. "Let's sit. I just want to talk to you for a few minutes and find out what your feelings are about all this."

Again Zack offered to leave but Lucy shook her head, wanting him to stay. He sat at the table with them. His presence was a reminder that he'd made all of this happen…that he'd helped her in an important way.

On the way in from the airport, they'd made conversation about the area and Gillian's life in L.A.. Now, Lucy explained how happy she'd always been with the McIntyres yet how she'd always felt part of her was missing. "If I can find my sister, maybe I'll feel more…whole," she finished.

Gillian seemed to assess what Lucy had said, then she turned her gaze on Zack. "Can you give us some time alone?"

A small protest must have escaped Lucy because Gillian looked at her kindly. "Energy is a funny thing. It can easily get blocked. The truth is that I'm feeling lots of it zipping back and forth between the two of you, and I'm afraid it's going to get in the way."

Gillian had just met her and Zack. She couldn't possibly know—

But Zack stood. "I'll be outside if you need me."

After the door closed, Gillian said, "I didn't mean to embarrass you. But you brought me here for a reason and I have to tell you what works and what doesn't. You have a strong connection to Zack and I needed him out of the way."

"You could feel that?"

"I could. When I was helping Nathan, I began falling for him. That muddled up what I was trying to do for him in searching for his daughters."

"How long have you been married?"

"Five years now. And I still feel like a newlywed," she admitted with a smile.

Lucy thought about Matthew in the other room and felt a little jealous. Could Gillian read her mind?

But Gillian seemed oblivious to what she was thinking. It seemed to be "connections" she tuned into.

"Show me the picture you mentioned," Gillian suggested.

Lucy took it from her pocket. She'd started carrying it with her.

Gillian studied it, then studied Lucy. "Hold my hand," Gillian directed her.

Lucy did.

Gillian closed her eyes. Then she opened them again. "I want you to think of your earliest memory. Take a little journey with me. Picture yourself around the age of ten. Can you envision what you're doing?"

A smile and a memory swept into her mind easily. "Marty and I are climbing the oak out back, knowing we were going to get into trouble for it." She felt the squeeze of Gillian's hand.

"That's good. Now think about what you were doing when you were about eight."

Letting her thoughts drift back, Lucy recalled, "Dad had trained a horse named Saddlebags just for me. She had markings liked saddlebags in white. I loved her so much. Mom thought I was too young but Dad let me ride her everyday and I always felt safe on her."

"That's great, Lucy. Now in your mind, drift back to photo albums your mom kept. Go back and back and back until you can see your baby pictures."

Lucy did, thinking about photos in the living room bookcase...of her standing beside Marty and Rick, their arms around her...of a tall Christmas tree—a tradition in their family...of a photo of her crawling under its branches. Then she thought about the photo on the table now.

"Stay in that picture," Gillian said quietly.

Suddenly, she squeezed Lucy's hand.

"What?" Lucy asked, her eyes popping open.

Gillian studied her for a few moments, then looked down at the photo, touching it. "Do you know anyone named Cassie? Cassidy?"

"No. Why?"

"Because that's the name that seems to be dancing all around you when you touch that photo...when you remember your baby pictures. Although you don't know your sister's name, there can still be a bond, energy connecting you because you're sisters. That energy can lead me in a certain direction. I'm getting a bunch of pictures that I'll need to sort out. I have to figure out what's here and now and what happened back then. Do you mind if I show Matthew the horses and just wander about the barns?"

"I don't mind at all. If there's anything at all that you need, don't hesitate to ask."

"I won't. I'll want to talk to my partner later so he can investigate what I think I have. Jake's good at the data-base detective work."

"So you think my sister's name is Cassidy?"

"Let me process this for a while. I'll talk to your family, too. Someone named Cassidy might have taken care of you when you were little."

But Lucy's parents weren't familiar with the name, either. So while Gillian processed, all Lucy could do was wait…and hope.

Late that evening, seated in the kitchen having a cup of tea with her mother and Gillian, Lucy watched Zack with Matthew. He was just as good with the four-year-old as he was with Josh. He'd make a wonderful dad.

Zack caught her watching him more than once as he read to Matthew. Each time their gazes locked. She vividly remembered everything that had happened in the barn. From the look on his face so did he. They hadn't talked about it yet. Lucy didn't want to talk about her being sterile because there was nothing she could do to change it.

When Gillian's phone beeped, Lucy jumped. Her nerves were getting to her.

Gillian checked the screen and said, "Be right back." As she went into the bedroom on the first floor for privacy, Lucy's heart raced.

Ten minutes later, Gillian returned to the kitchen, smiling. "Jake has worked his magic. He found a Cassidy Sullivan listed in a Cheyenne database. Her age checks out. He found out some other things, too, as he dug around. She went through the foster care system in

Laramie and was never adopted. Apparently she was in some trouble as a teenager—something about hot-wiring a car. But records indicate she inherited Twin Pines ranch near Cheyenne and is now living there." Gillian handed Lucy a piece of paper where a number was written. "We, of course, don't know if this is her. But it feels right."

Obviously overhearing some of it, Zack left Matthew turning the pages of his book and joined them. He said to Gillian, "I know you go through a process when you do this. Tell Lucy why this name and background feel right. It might ease her apprehension a little."

After a quick glance at him, Gillian nodded. "When we were talking this afternoon and I saw Cassie's name, I felt as if I was seeing a ranch, too. But I didn't know if it was this one or another. And as I met your horses and toured the Rising Star, I realized this wasn't the ranch I was seeing. Those twin pines that Cassie's ranch is named after stand on either side of a huge arch that leads into the ranch. When Jake checked Google images, he could see them and the arch. I'm pretty sure this is your sister, Lucy. But the only way you'll know for certain is if you call."

Lucy's mom wrapped her arm around her. "We can't tell you what to do, honey. Just know that we'll be here for you, no matter what you decide and no matter what happens. You are our daughter and nothing will ever change that."

Tears welled up in Lucy's eyes as she returned her mother's hug. "I'm going to try to call her now. I've been so nervous about this all day. I just want to know."

Her mother said, "I'll go tell your father and Marty what's happened. You go to your room for some privacy. Go on now."

Matthew chose that moment to run into the kitchen with his book. "Look, Mommy! Another horse. Can I have a horse?"

Gillian gazed down at her son with that adoring look a mom gives her child. "Why don't you talk to Daddy about it when we get home."

"I will," Matthew assured her with a vigorous nod.

Lucy really liked this woman who might have given her her sister. "Thank you," she said with all the gratitude in her heart.

"Don't thank me yet. See what comes of your phone call. Remember, don't expect too much. This could be a real shock for both of you."

Zack followed Lucy to the stairs. "Are you okay?"

"I will be. I just have to know."

He ran his hand down the side of her cheek. When he did, all the electricity Gillian must have felt humming between them crackled around them. Lucy briefly touched her hand to his and then climbed the steps.

Lucy's hands felt sweaty as she sat on the side of her bed, her cell phone in her hand. She stared at the number for a few seconds and then she pressed it in and hit SEND.

Someone picked up on the second ring.

"Twin Pines Ranch." It was a woman's voice.

"Is Cassidy Sullivan there?" Lucy asked, holding her breath.

"I'm Cassidy Sullivan."

"My name is Lucy McIntyre. I…" Lucy didn't know how to say it except just to say it. "I think I'm your sister. The lawyer who handled my adoption came into some information recently and that's how we found you. I'm not sure exactly how to go about this, but it was important for me to talk to you, to find out one way or another if you are my sister."

There was utter silence on the other end of the line and Lucy's heart almost stopped.

"We're sisters?" Cassidy asked.

"Maybe even twins. When were you born?"

"August third, 1985."

"It's the same as mine! It's even possible we're identical."

Again, the silence worried Lucy. Maybe Cassidy Sullivan didn't want a sister or care if she had one.

Finally, Cassidy said softly, "I've never had any real family."

"Do you have a photo you could email me?" Lucy asked. "I can do the same."

Cassidy hesitated. "My computer is down right now. I have a fax, though. Can you fax me your photo? Let me give you my fax number. By the way, just call me Cassie. I don't use Cassidy much. Where do you live?"

"In Long Brush." Cheyenne was three hours away.

"I can't get away from the ranch right now," Cassie said regretfully. "I'm short-handed. Could you possibly come here? I have plenty of room if you'd like to stay a few days."

Relief flooded through Lucy. "I'd like that."

Cassie asked. "Are you married?"

"No."

"I was just thinking if you don't want to make the drive alone, bring somebody with you. Do you have family?"

Cassie's questions gave Lucy hope that she wanted to know more about her in the same way Lucy wanted to know all about Cassie's life. After Lucy explained her adoption, they talked for almost a half-hour as Lucy decided she'd drive to Cheyenne the following day.

When she hung up the phone, she realized she had talked to Cassie so easily she already felt connected to her. Could they really be twins?

Returning to the kitchen, she saw her dad and Marty were there now along with her mom, Zack and Gillian. Everyone stared at her expectantly.

"I'm going to fax her my photo and she's going to do the same. I'm going to drive there tomorrow," she said, fully expecting to go alone.

But her father frowned.

"What's the matter, Dad?"

"I want you to meet your sister and as soon as you can. But a front's supposed to move in and the weather might turn bad late tomorrow."

"I'm going to stay overnight."

"Will I be able to fly out in the morning?" Gillian asked.

"You should be okay if you leave early. But later it's supposed to sleet, maybe snow," her father explained. "I don't know, Lucy—"

"I can go with you if you like," Zack offered.

All heads swung toward him.

"Unless you need me here," he clarified.

"That's a wonderful idea!" Esther said.

Tom agreed with a shake of his head. "You can take my 4x4."

Marty kept silent.

Lucy thought about waiting, but once weather like that moved in, it might not break for a few days. Meeting her sister had become a need she didn't want to deny. Especially after talking to Cassie, she didn't want to wait any longer than necessary to see her, to really get to know her.

Then she thought about the ride there with Zack.

"Won't you be bored?" she asked him. "I don't know what I'm going to be doing. Cassie and I might just sit around talking."

"If she lives on a ranch, there will be plenty to do. I won't get bored. Now if you don't trust my driving ability—"

"I'm not worried about your driving."

Everyone was obviously waiting to find out what she *was* worried about. Since she wasn't about to talk about *that*, she agreed. "If you're sure you want to come, that's fine." Lucy turned to Gillian and hugged her. "I don't know how to repay you."

"Just build a good relationship with your sister. That's repayment enough."

Her family stood then and each of them had something to say to her. Her dad said, "Don't expect too much too fast. This might take a little time. Even though you're sisters, you're strangers."

"I know," Lucy said with a smile.

Her mother gave her a hug. "Don't ever be afraid of telling us anything, Lucy. We're your parents and we'll help you through whatever it is."

Lucy glanced over at Marty who was looking on. She wished he could really hear her parent's words, admit he needed help, and believe that they would all stand by him, too.

After the others had moved away, he crossed to her and asked. "You won't move away will you, Lucy? I mean if you get along with her and everything, and she's really your sister…"

"*You* are really my brother, and I'm not going anywhere, except for a visit."

Unlike the others Zack didn't say anything to her, but went into the living room with the men and sat by the fireplace. She went to find a photo to fax to Cassie Sullivan, hoping they looked a little alike—hoping they truly *were* twins.

Lucy stood in her father's office in the barn, just staring at Cassie Sullivan's photo. They were twins! Possibly identical twins. They looked so much alike no one could deny it.

Lucy heard the barn door open. Expecting her dad or mom, she was surprised when Zack stood in the office doorway.

She showed him the picture without saying a word. "So there's no doubt."

"No doubt at all," she agreed.

"Are you going to be able to sleep tonight?" he asked gently.

"Probably not. I'm too excited." Standing beside her, his vest topping his flannel shirt, she could feel his body heat. And hers.

"You *should* be excited. Do you want to leave around 7:30?"

"That sounds good." She found herself excited about driving to Cheyenne with him in addition to meeting Cassie. "Thank you for offering to drive. I know I could do it myself, but your offer will make my parents feel better about it."

After studying her a few moments, he asked, "What about you? You didn't seem too eager to accept."

The other evening in the barn clearly flashed in her mind. "I didn't want you to be in an awkward position if you didn't really want to be with me."

His blue eyes going a deeper blue, he clasped her shoulder. "I do want to be with you, Lucy. Don't have any doubts about that. But we can talk about that tomorrow. We'll have plenty of time."

The welcome heat of his hand on her shoulder ceased as he stepped away from her. She wished for plenty of time with Zack, to explore everything she felt about him. If he was determined to leave, her inability to have children might not matter to him. But did that mean she was simply convenient?

Too many confusing thoughts swirled in her head and she hoped in the next few days she might be able to sort some of them out.

Chapter Ten

After a breakfast of bacon, eggs and pancakes, after hugs and "keep in touch" all around, Lucy watched Rick drive Gillian and Matthew off to the airport while she and Zack headed for the road to Cheyenne. The sky was grey and the air damply frigid. But neither rain, nor sleet, nor snow was falling and they wanted to make as much time as they could before it did. Zack didn't speak until he turned onto the main highway.

As the sound of the tires became a lulling monotony, he glanced at Lucy. "We need to talk about what happened in the barn."

Although she'd told herself she was prepared, although she'd expected him to bring it up, she really wasn't ready. Too many feelings were bumping around inside of her. She could avoid this discussion, at least postpone it, or face it head on.

"What do we need to discuss?" she asked quietly.

"Your reaction...my reaction. Why we stopped."

After drawing in a deep breath, she plunged in. "We stopped because I laid a bomb in your lap."

"Not exactly in my lap." His smile was wry.

Even that smile of his could steal her breath. "I know how men feel about this subject." It was difficult to keep the sadness from her voice.

He shot her a perplexed look. "Which subject are we discussing? Sex or having children?"

"Having children. Pete broke off our relationship when he found out that I couldn't."

Zack swore. "You're *not* serious."

"I'm *very* serious. He didn't want a wife who couldn't bear him children, and I have the feeling that's how a lot of men feel."

Without any hesitation, Zack protested. "I don't know about a lot of men, Lucy, but the right one wouldn't care. As you already know, adoption can be a wonderful thing, too."

"Maybe." More than anything, she wanted Zack to be the right man. But she knew until he faced his grief, he wouldn't be ready to love again. Sometimes grief didn't fade. It made a permanent home in your heart like an old friend.

Even so, she had to ask the question. "Are you saying you could marry a woman who *couldn't* have children?"

This time he was slow to answer. "I don't think about marrying again."

"But if you did, how would you feel?"

Several revolutions of the tires passed time until he responded, "I could adopt children and accept them as my own."

Was he trying to make her feel better or did he really believe it? Sometimes theory sounded better than actual practice. And something else bothered her. "If you're not interested in marriage, then you're only interested in sex."

"I'm interested in what's happening between us. I don't think it's purely physical, do you?"

"But if you intend to leave—"

"I intend to leave."

The silence in the car echoed his words. "Then it's better nothing did happen the other night," she murmured without anger but with great disappointment.

After their discussion, there didn't seem to be any more to say. Eventually Zack switched on the radio to easy listening music that filled the car along with their thoughts.

Two hours later, they stopped at a gas station for coffee. They'd no sooner gotten back on the road and picked up speed when tiny pings of sleet pestered the windshield.

"I was hoping for snow instead," Zack muttered. "It would be easier to navigate."

The ice fell on and off at first, then in a steady spitting stream that thankfully still melted on the road. But as they proceeded further, they could hear the crunch of it under their tires and Zack slowed. "It will just take us longer to get there. Good thing I didn't bring the Harley."

He was trying to ease the tension between them, but Lucy's heart was heavy with the knowledge that he would leave sooner rather than later. She was also becoming more anxious about the woman she'd find when she reached Twin Pines. Just who was Cassie Sullivan? She sounded kind. She seemed to love horses as much as Lucy. But did she?

Zack's hands were firm on the steering wheel, his attention focused on the road ahead, when a beat-up truck passed them like a bat out of hell. The problem was the truck lost traction swerving back into the right lane and almost clipped Zack. Only Zack's quick reaction saved them from an accident. But as he spun the steering wheel, they skidded off the side of the road into the brush. Zack braked sharply, jolting both of them. The truck stalled.

His curse was long and loud but then he looked over at Lucy. "Are you okay?"

She felt shaken, but she said, "I'm fine. How about you?"

Unsnapping his seat belt, he then unfastened hers. "Move around a little," he ordered. "See if anything hurts."

"Really, Zack…"

"Humor me, Lucy."

She did as he asked. "I'm okay. Do you think the roads are so bad that we have to stop?"

His face was close to hers, his brow furrowed. "Do you want to stop?"

"No, but I also don't want to jeopardize our lives or Dad's truck."

When Zack clasped her shoulder, she felt all the things she'd felt the other night in the barn…and more. "Then we'll keep going as long as we can."

Slipping his arm around her, he brought her close

for a hug. It could have just been a hug. But the embrace went long and neither of them moved away. He lifted her chin up and kissed her. The kiss was quick and hot and over before it could become a distraction that kept them along the side of the road. But it heated Lucy's cheeks and warmed her insides and left her tingling and wanting more.

After they buckled up again, he turned the key and the truck jumped to life. Carefully he drove them back onto the road and headed toward Cheyenne.

By the time they reached the entrance to Twin Pines with a tall pine standing at either side of the high wooden arch, they were only doing about 25 miles an hour. The lane leading to the ranch was lined with iced pines that shimmered silver. Because the lane was slipperier than the main road had been, they slid to an imperfect stop before a rambling three-story house. Covered with Wedgwood blue siding, it was accented with black shutters. The wide porch wrapped around the house like an apron.

"Stay put until I come around for you," Zack ordered.

They could see the ice had created a slick coating on the sidewalk and the porch rail. Lucy wasn't exactly sure what Zack had in mind until she opened her door.

When he lifted her out, her arm automatically swung around his neck. Her fingertips grazed the hair on his nape and he held her a little tighter. Then he carried her carefully up the steps.

Setting her down in front of the door, he encouraged, "Go ahead and knock. I'll get our bags."

With her heart pounding, her body still tingling from being held in his strong arms, Lucy opened the storm door and rapped on the wooden door inside.

It opened immediately and the two women stared at each other. It was like looking at a mirror image, Lucy thought! Except Cassie's hair was longer and she wore it in a pony tail. But the set of her eyes, the straightness of her nose, the curve of her mouth were all the same as Lucy's.

Cassie took Lucy's hand and pulled her inside. "I can't believe it. You look just like me!"

They both laughed and then they were hugging. Tears of joy filled Lucy's eyes and she let them fall. She only vaguely heard the storm door open again.

"I was so worried about you," Cassie said as she leaned away. "I heard the roads are terrible."

Although still engrossed in her sister, Lucy sensed Zack standing nearby. "I'd like you to meet someone. Zackary Burke, my twin sister Cassie Sullivan."

Cassie extended her hand to Zack. "Hello, it's nice to meet you. I'm glad Lucy didn't make this trip alone, especially with the weather today."

After they'd shaken hands, Cassie said, "Take off your coats. I have lunch ready. I'm afraid afterwards, I'm going to have to see to chores. My foreman is sick with the flu. Two of the other men in the bunkhouse have it, too."

"I can help you," Lucy offered.

But Cassie shook her head. "You're a guest."

Zack suggested easily, "If we all help, you'll have more time with Lucy."

Though Cassie still protested, she seemed pleased at their offer.

As an observer, Zack saw the likenesses between the women as well as the differences. They indeed did look alike, but Lucy had a dimple to the left of her mouth when she smiled. Cassie didn't. And Cassie had a few more freckles. Lucy's hair wasn't quite as dark, but her eyes were darker. No surprise to Zack because of the studies he'd read about twins, they had many of the same mannerisms—the flutter of a hand when they were excited about what they were talking about, a certain tilt to their heads as they listened. They talked practically non-stop through lunch about the Rising Star and Twin Pines and how their ranches differed. Twin Pines was larger and they ran cattle instead of raising horses. Instead of a training arena, there was a bunkhouse with a kitchen attached for the hired hands…only one barn where they kept horses and a cabin for guests. But Cassie, like Lucy, would ride any chance she got. And her best friend? A horse named Delilah.

"I usually have a housekeeper, too," Cassie explained. "But Rachel is visiting relatives in Montana. I guess you're wondering how I came into all this," Cassie said, looking at Lucy.

"It's none of my business unless you want to tell me," Lucy answered.

As if she'd had to explain many times, Cassie shrugged. "It's no secret. When our mother died, I went in to foster care but was never adopted. Some of the people wanted to take in foster kids to get money and to have help with chores. I just didn't fit in. I got into a lot of trouble as a teenager. At seventeen I'd finally had enough of the foster system and decided to run away. I hot-wired a car and had made it to Cheyenne when I was in an accident. I was pretty seriously hurt."

Zack and Lucy exchanged a look. Cassie had been in an accident at the same age as Lucy!

Cassie went on, "But I had a wonderful social worker and she knew the owner of Twin Pines—Tina Christopher. Tina took me in and became my mentor. She became everything I never had. She gave me a real home and a place to belong, and when she died two years ago, she left me everything. I'm going to spend the rest of my days making sure Twin Pines is a success."

Zack saw the look in Lucy's eyes that said she could only begin to imagine what her twin had gone through.

Without hesitation, Lucy took her sister's hand. "I'm so glad I found you. I can't wait for you to meet my family."

Cassie looked as if she was fighting emotion. Her voice caught when she said, "I'd like that."

According to plan, they all worked together that afternoon, sharing the chores in the barn. Lucy and Cassie chattered whenever they got within a foot of each other. They had so much to say and didn't seem to mind if Zack listened. Every once in a while, they'd stop and study each other again in amazement and then hug. Zack's heart began to ache and he wasn't sure exactly why.

Supper was a simple meal of broiled burgers and baked potatoes. Cassie explained she cooked to get by but not much else. Lucy explained how her mother had taught her everything about cooking ever since she was old enough to stand on the stool and watch her, and if Cassie was interested, she'd be glad to teach her anything she wanted to know. But Cassie just shrugged and said she usually didn't have time for cooking, so Lucy let the subject drop.

When the women went into the living room after dinner, Zack suddenly felt as if he needed space and lots of it. "I'm going to get some air," he said, reaching for his coat that had landed over an old rocker.

"It's wet and cold out there, Zack," Lucy protested.

"I'm not foolish enough to venture from the porch. I won't be long."

He didn't wait for her to call after him. Conversation was the last thing he wanted. The ice and frigid temperature might numb everything he didn't want to feel. The bond Lucy was forming with Cassie made him that much more aware of his lack of bonds and family.

After he went outside, he stood against the house, one booted foot propped behind him on the wall. The grass, the walk, the truck and the buildings were all covered with at least a half inch of ice. Wet snow and sleet still fell, and he stared into it, searching for answers. Watching Lucy and Cassie together gave him the same tight feeling in his chest that being with the McIntyre clan had. Intellectually he realized bonds were a good thing. But sometimes the pain of severing them was too great to be borne. He remembered the loneliness and fear of being uprooted from a familiar place, the ranch he and his parents had loved. He still remembered the feelings of desolation when his parents had died. Eventually he'd learned how to get along without getting connected. After all, the connections would soon enough be broken. As an adult, he'd concentrated on his studies, med school, and then his practice. He was the kind of doctor who knew how to listen and his patients liked him.

When he'd met Kay, he'd liked her immediately. They hadn't experienced grand passion but they'd shared common interests. She'd been smart, schooled, and an excellent conversationalist. Her lawyer's mind was analytical and she didn't want to make him her world. They'd suited each other, and Zack had thought he'd finally put down roots. When she became pregnant, he'd embraced the idea of fatherhood wholeheartedly.

He never should have taken her on that camping trip! She'd been insistent, needing to get away for a few days, she'd said, reminding him that once the baby was born, time alone would be very scarce. They'd had a common enjoyment in camping, escaping the hustle and bustle of over-busy lives. But he should have known better.

Standing there on the porch, he wasn't aware of the passing of time or the wind or the cold. He'd been cold inside for so long. And the thought of Christmas…

When the door opened, he stood still.

Lucy was bundled in her coat and looked concerned. "Aren't you getting cold out here?"

"I'm fine, Lucy. Go back in." His voice was terse and strained.

But she didn't do as he said. He was far enough away from the porch light that he knew she couldn't see him well in the shadows and right now he just wanted to keep her away. "I don't want company."

Hesitating a moment, finally she crossed to him. "What's wrong?"

"Nothing's wrong! I needed fresh air."

"This is frigid air and the only reason you might want to still be out here is to numb something that might be thawing."

"I don't need a psychologist," he snapped.

"What you need is a friend. I can be that if you let me."

She was so damn stubborn sometimes. "A friend won't help. Nothing will help. I lost my wife and I lost my child and nothing will ever bring them back." He couldn't believe the vehement bitterness in just saying it.

Coming closer, Lucy looked up at him. "No, nothing will ever bring them back."

It was as if someone else saying the words finally made their deaths much too real. Zack felt his throat constricting and his eyes stinging and he turned away from her to stare into the dark night.

She moved in front of him again and took his cold face between her warm hands. "Zack, you have to let yourself feel it. You have to feel the grief before you can ever get over it. You loved them, both your wife and your unborn child. You can't just put that love on a shelf. You can't deny it existed. And you can't deny that you exist with the memories."

"I don't *want* to feel it. I don't want to—" His voice caught and Lucy wrapped her arms around him.

Lucy was warmth and desire. Her name which he

knew meant "light" said it all. She was becoming his light. Her caring made him remember too many things—his wife's embrace, holidays with laughter, his mother's hugs. Tears he'd never shed slipped down his face…and he felt like a complete fool.

Wrenching away, he let the cold numb him again. He couldn't let Lucy see him like this. In the past two years, he'd gotten his life back under control.

But since he'd met Lucy—

"In a few short weeks, you've stirred up everything I *never* wanted to feel again. Go inside," he ordered curtly. "I don't need you, and I want you to leave me alone."

He saw the hurt on Lucy's face and felt it keenly in his soul. But he couldn't let her in and he couldn't let his feelings out. He might feel an attraction toward her, but it wasn't worth the pain it would bring.

This time she didn't argue with him. She turned away and went in the house.

But as Zack tried to see through the darkness, his eyes burned and he realized taking the job at the Rising Star had opened a Pandora's box that he might never be able to close again.

Because Zack was in pain, Lucy wanted to stay with him. She wanted to put her arms around him and help him deal with his grief. But her mother had been right. He didn't want to feel weak in front of her, and he got angry when he did.

After she took off her coat, she went into the living room.

Cassie looked up. "Everything all right?" she asked.

Lucy shook her head. "Zack has some things to work through."

"Are you two involved?"

"Zack hired on about a month ago and he's become one of the family. But I don't think he wants to *be* one of the family."

"I'm not sure that answers my question."

Lowering herself on the rocker near the fireplace, cold from more than the frigid weather outside, she explained, "Zack's running from losses in his life. He says he's not going to stay at the Rising Star."

"But you're in love with him, aren't you?" Cassie asked gently.

"Is it so obvious?"

"No, not obvious. But I can see it in the way you look at him, the way you talk about him."

"How about you?" Lucy asked. "Is there someone special in your life?"

Cassie immediately shook her head. "No."

As she and Cassie continued to talk about how far Twin Pines was from town and the lack of eligible men, Lucy listened for the door. Finally it opened and she heard Zack come inside. It was getting late and Cassie showed them to their rooms upstairs—she had insisted they stay in the main house. Zack's room was next to Lucy's. His attitude toward her was remote and as he crossed the threshold into his room, he bid them both a polite good-night.

Cassie gave her a hug and murmured, "It will work out."

As Lucy stepped into her room, she hoped that was true. But she had a feeling "working out" might mean never seeing Zack again.

As Lucy readied herself for bed, she was aware of movement beyond the wall. The wood floor creaked as Zack moved about and she sat on the bed listening. She heard the fall of his boots, the clatter of a belt against a chair and finally the squeak of a bed. Unbidden she remembered Zack's bare chest, the hair on it, the way his skin had felt under her fingers, the passion he'd stirred up that she'd never imagine she'd feel. There was such a longing to be with him in the most intimate way possible. But if he didn't trust her to see his grief, she didn't know if they could ever have true intimacy.

Swiftly, she donned her nightgown and slipped under the covers. Maybe tomorrow would bring some answers…maybe tomorrow he'd let her in.

In the barn the next morning, Zack helped Cassie take care of the horses. Lucy had insisted on making breakfast. A layer of ice coated the countryside. With the temperature too cold for it to melt, Zack wondered if the power lines could handle the weight. He'd planned to go exploring while Lucy visited with Cassie, but the roads were still too treacherous to attempt it.

"I saw your wood pile is running low out back. After breakfast I'll split some logs for you."

"Loren, my foreman, usually takes care of that, but he was still looking pretty weak when I checked on him this morning. I could have one of the other hands do it, though. It's not your responsibility, Zack."

"I don't mind. Besides, I need something to keep me busy."

"Have you always been a cowboy?" Cassie asked with a smile.

He stopped scooping feed into the horses' trough. "Why do you ask?"

"You just seem city-born and bred to me."

"I'm a little of both. This change of life style was a…conscious choice."

"You don't give much away, do you?"

"I like to keep my life private."

"We all do, but we can't always do that."

Zack sensed the same strength in Cassie he often felt emanating from Lucy and he was curious about this wild teenager that inherited and now ran a sizable ranch. "How many head do you run here?" he asked.

She accepted his change of subject and told him. As they finished their chores, they discussed the size of Twin Pines and everything involved in keeping it running smoothly. "I couldn't do it without Loren," Cassie confessed. "He started working for Tina when he was a teenager and still knows this place better than I do."

"Are you computerized?" Zack asked.

Cassie nodded, but quickly said, "Loren takes care of all that. I'd rather be on horseback or tending to the cattle." Closing the lid on the feed bin, she zipped up her jacket. "We better get up to the house for breakfast or it will be too cold to eat."

After breakfast, Zack split wood while Cassie and Lucy cleaned tack and continued to talk. He noticed they never seemed to run out of things to say. There was tension between him and Lucy that he knew he had caused but he didn't know how to make it go away.

He worked throughout the day finding chores to occupy him until finally before supper, he asked Cassie, "Do you have books or magazines I could page through?"

"In my office," she said. "C'mon, I'll show you." Down a short hall from the kitchen, she showed him into a room with a massive wooden desk and a computer sitting on its top. She pointed to a pile of magazines in one corner. "There might be something there."

"Do you have *Wyoming Country*?" he asked.

She looked unsettled for a moment. "You'll have to look."

Going over to the corner, he picked up a few. The ad on the back of one caught his attention. It was for a new kind of feed for livestock.

"Ever use this?" he asked.

Cassie looked at the page but her expression was blank. "Um, I don't think so," she said.

"Tom, Lucy's father, says he thinks the horses have stayed healthier since he's been buying it." When he offered her the magazine, she shrugged and didn't take it. "I pretty much stick to what I know works well. Just make yourself at home in here. I'll go help Lucy."

Zack wondered why Cassie had skittered out of the

office so quickly. It didn't seem in character. Something about her office seemed odd to him and then he figured out what it was. Most offices had bulletin boards with memos, papers lying about, schedules or calendars on the wall. This one didn't. And he wondered if Cassie was just particularly neat or if there was a reason.

But it was none of his business. He settled in the living room with the magazines while the women made supper.

That evening the wind howled outside. Zack was edgy and needed something to keep him occupied...something other than thinking about Lucy, about kissing her, about leaving. "I have a deck of cards in my duffel. How about a game?"

"I'm not good at cards," Cassie said. "Why don't you and Lucy play? I sketch in my spare time and I'd like to do one of Lucy so that I have it. I can work on it while you play."

At Lucy's nod, Zack went upstairs to get the deck and brought it down to the living room. He and Lucy settled on the floor by the coffee table and decided on gin. The problem was with just the two of them playing, their eyes met often, their fingers brushed accidentally now and then. Every time it happened, Zack was aware of the electricity between them. Cassie had turned on soft music in the background and conversation was minimal.

They took a break from their game mid evening to have hot chocolate, but then returned to it. When they did, Zack asked Lucy, "When are you planning to go back home?"

She looked over at Cassie. "I hate to leave, but I really

do need to get back. Rick's leaving for Fort Worth day after tomorrow. I listened to the news earlier and the ice is supposed to melt tomorrow. What if we leave after lunch?"

"Fine by me," Zack commented.

"Cassie, do you think you could get away and come spend Christmas with us? I know my family would love to have you."

"I'll talk to Loren about it and see what he says. He has a nephew in Vermont and sometimes he spends the holidays with him."

After a few more strokes with her pencil, Cassie lifted the sketch she'd drawn and said to Lucy, "What do you think?"

The likeness was striking and Zack automatically said, "You have talent."

Cassie shrugged. "I always liked to draw. It's just a hobby."

"Like Lucy's wood carving."

As Lucy explained about her work room and the type of carving she did, Zack collected the cards. "I'm going to turn in. With that wind howling, it might take a while to get to sleep." At the foot of the steps, he wished them good night.

Lucy's eyes locked to his. "Good night, Zack."

Everything about Lucy seemed to haunt him now. The sound of her voice echoed in his head. He could picture her without even conjuring her up. As he showered, he tried to let the water wash her from his consciousness. But when he emerged from the bathroom in jeans and his open flannel shirt, she was coming down the hall.

She stopped at the doorway to her bedroom, and

Zack couldn't keep from approaching her. "Is you visit going the way you hoped?"

"Better than I ever hoped," she admitted with a smile. "Cassie and I don't know much about each other yet, not really, but I do feel as if she's my sister."

There was an awkward silence between them.

"Lucy, about last night…"

She remained quiet, not helping him at all.

"I didn't mean to be harsh to you."

"At that moment, yes, you did. You didn't want me anywhere near you."

"I'm trying to apologize."

"For what? Feeling grief? Or not wanting me to see it? Neither needs an apology, Zack. I just wish you'd understand that I won't think less of you if you let me see your pain."

He raked his hand through his hair. "You're pushing me. You're making me feel, and I don't like it."

Tilting her head, she gazed into his eyes. "You make me feel, too."

It was such a simple statement with so much truth that he slid his hand along her neck and wove his fingers into her hair. "Maybe we should decide just to feel the *good* things," he murmured as he bent his head to hers and set his lips on her mouth.

But before the kiss could become a temptingly more intimate kiss, she pushed away. "What good things do you want to feel, Zack? Are we talking about pleasure or more?"

Swearing, he shook his head. "Can't you just take this chemistry for what it is and go with it?"

"No. Because I think you're searching for more than chemistry and just don't know it."

He stepped back, shaken by the thought. "Just because you found a long-lost sister is no reason to think I want more than I've already got. When you're ready to admit your desire matches mine, you let me know. Just realize, Lucy, desire is all I've got to give."

Then he went to his room and shut the door.

Chapter Eleven

After lunch the following day, Zack drank a second cup of coffee while Lucy packed her things.

Cassie was sitting across the table from him and she said, "You seem a million miles away."

"Not that far."

The sound of a truck outside forestalled further comment as Cassie rose and went to the door. The ice had melted throughout the sunny morning and Zack was glad the weather was clear for the drive home. He glimpsed the red, white and blue insignia of a mail truck as the carrier ran up the porch steps and handed a bundle to Cassie. She thanked him and brought it inside laying it on the table, not seemingly interested in what was there. She started putting the dishes from their lunch into the dishwasher.

He didn't know what made him ask, but he nodded to the stack of letters. "Aren't you going to sort through it?"

Cassie glanced at him. "Later."

He realized now what had struck him as odd about the house. Just as in her office, there were no magazines scattered about, no brochures, no newspapers, nothing in print. There was a calendar hanging over by the sink with red x's in the blocks up until today's date. He took a stab in the dark, "What day is Christmas on this year?"

He pointed to the calendar that was too far away for him to see. Cassie went over to it and with her back to him, he could have sworn she counted the x's.

Standing, he crossed to her and saw her finger trailing along the blocks. When she looked up at him, she seemed almost scared.

"Cassie, can you tell me what day Christmas lands on without counting?"

She shook her head slowly.

"You can't read, can you?" he asked softly.

She looked as if she were going to deny the fact but then she shook her head. "No, I can't. I have dyslexia." She clasped his arm. "Please don't tell Lucy."

"Why not? I'm sure she'd understand."

"It's a secret I've kept all these years. Only Loren knows. He reads me whatever is necessary, takes care of the computer work. Please, Zack, don't say anything."

Zack could see her shame and her fear. But before he could soothe either, Lucy came into the kitchen and saw Cassie's hand on his arm. There were questions in her eyes.

Cassie dropped her hand as he said to Lucy, "We were counting the days until Christmas. There aren't many left."

Lucy set her bag by the door. "That's why I have to get back. There's a lot to do."

Cassie left Zack's side to go to her sister. "I'll let you know about Christmas as soon as I can. I'd like to come and meet your family, but if Loren leaves to spend Christmas with Ben, I'll have to stay at the ranch."

Lucy nodded. "I understand. In the meantime, we can email and call."

"I'm not big on letters," Cassie said. "I like the phone much better. Can you give me a call when you get home so I know you arrived safely?"

"Sure, I will."

The two sisters studied each other again and then hugged.

After Zack picked up Lucy's bag, he followed the women onto the porch.

For the most part, Zack and Lucy's drive back to the Rising Star was quiet. And the next few days weren't much different. Zack went his way and Lucy went hers.

One evening when Zack came in from working, Lucy was sitting at the kitchen table talking to her mother about Cassie and how much she wanted her to come over Christmas.

Esther had asked, "Do you think if I invited her, too, it will help?"

Lucy had smiled and said, "It wouldn't hurt." But when her gaze had met Zack's, her smile had faded away.

Thursday morning he saw her drive off in her car. Esther explained she was going to run errands for the family and spend the day Christmas shopping. But when snow unexpectedly began to fall around noon, Zack watched for her car on the road every half hour. By two o'clock the snow was piling up. By four o'clock there was at least four inches. And no call from Lucy. By six o'clock, Zack was worried.

After supper, as if trying to forestall her own concern, Esther said to him, "All cell phone service is spotty around here, especially when the weather acts up. Lucy has friends in town. Maybe she'll decide to stay overnight with one of them."

"Then she should have called," he muttered. "There's six inches of snow out there."

Esther patted his arm. "We'll call the chief of police in Long Brush and give him her car's description. We know Jeff and he'll radio his deputies to keep a lookout. I'm sure she'll either call or walk in that door any minute now. Come on and have another piece of pie and stop worrying."

But when Tom picked up the phone to call the police chief, he frowned. "Service is out now. The weight of the snow must have gotten the lines again. No wonder we haven't heard from Lucy. With the phone lines down, I can't even email. Maybe we should get one of those SAT phones. It might be worth the expense."

Zack wished he had thought about buying a SAT phone long before now! He wanted to get in the truck and go into town after her himself, but he knew that would be ridiculous. He had no idea where to look. Still, Long Brush wasn't that big.

"I could take the truck," Zack said.

"Lucy said if she couldn't find what she wanted in Long Brush, she was going to drive to Chester. There are a few unique shops there. There's no telling where she is, Zack. We're just going to have to wait and trust that she's all right."

Trust. He didn't have any of that.

He paced most of the evening, going to the window and looking out, or standing outside on the porch as the snow mounted deeper and deeper. Even Marty looked worried. But Esther insisted that Lucy had good sense and would use it.

It was nine when the McIntyres climbed the stairs to reassure each other about Lucy, to read possibly, but probably not sleep. Zack knew he wasn't going to sleep, either, unless the phone rang or Lucy walked in the door. Since cable reception was disturbed, too, he couldn't surf the channels on the TV, so he stared into the dying flames of the fire.

He was thinking about everything he'd said to Lucy and things she'd said to him when he heard a noise on the porch. Jumping up, he crossed to the door and swung it open.

Lucy was snow-covered and shivering, even though she wore gloves, boots, and her hood was tied around her face.

When she stumbled inside, he took her by the shoulders. "What happened?"

Her teeth were chattering. "I followed a snow plow

but then…" Suddenly her shivering became worse and he knew there'd be time for explanations later.

"Let me help you." He untied the string under her chin and unzipped her coat. Her gloves were caked with snow and she had trouble pulling them off. He grabbed one and then the other, taking her hands between his.

"You're like ice," he mumbled, really worried. Hypothermia was the diagnosis that swept through his mind. He had to raise her core temperature. Her jeans were wet and soaked through. "I'm going to tell your family you're home and get you a change of clothes. I'll be right back."

Zack took the stairs two at a time and stopped at the first door. He knocked on the door and called in to Esther and Tom's room, "Lucy's home. She's cold but she's okay."

Esther came to the door and opened it. "Thank goodness. I'll come down and make her some hot chocolate."

For some reason, Zack didn't want everyone bustling around right now. He wanted to take care of Lucy himself. "I'll make the hot chocolate for her. But I wondered if you could find me some clothes. She needs to change out of her wet jeans."

With a knowing look, Esther smiled. "All right. Let me get her sweatsuit." A few minutes later, she came out of Lucy's room carrying pink sweat pants and a sweatshirt, then she called down the stairs.

"Lucy, are you all right?"

"Yes, Mom, I'm fine." Her voice sounded weaker than usual but it was a good effort.

Esther called down again. "Zack said he's going to make you hot chocolate. If you need anything, you come get me."

"Okay, Mom."

After hanging Lucy's clothes over Zack's arm, Esther smiled at him. "I know you'll take good care of her."

When Zack returned downstairs, he saw Lucy still sitting on the kitchen chair, shivering. She looked up at him. "I was too tired to move."

He handed her the clothes. "Go to my room and change, then we'll get you warmed up. Hot chocolate or tea?"

"Hot chocolate," she said, rising to her feet and taking the clothes from him.

Zack decided he'd give her ten minutes and if she wasn't back by then, he'd go check on her. Just as he poured the chocolate into two mugs, she walked down the hall, looking innocent, vulnerable, and sweet in the pink outfit. Her cheeks were still red from the cold and her hair was mussed and all he wanted to do was take her in his arms and kiss her. Instead he picked up the two mugs and carried them to the sofa. She followed and sat in the corner. He took the afghan from the back and covered her with it, sitting beside her. After she'd had a few sips of hot chocolate, she shivered then snuggled deeper under the cover.

The firelight flickered on her face as she said, "I'm still so cold."

Shifting closer to her, he draped his arm around her shoulders. "Let's combine body heat. You'll get warm quicker." Her head was almost on his chest. "Tell me what happened."

After another sip of chocolate, she explained, "I had driven to Chester this afternoon, right when it started snowing. I should have known better, I guess. But I wasn't nearly finished shopping and Chester has a few stores I like."

He waited.

"I was inside one of them for so long, I didn't realize what was happening outside. I tried to call but couldn't get through. Maybe if I had a fancier phone—" She sighed. "I know it was foolish to try to drive home, but I didn't want everyone to worry. I managed to get behind a plow on the main road and I was doing okay, though it was really slow going. I should have known I couldn't make it up the lane in this much snow. I got stuck in a drift and had to walk."

Zack's arm tightened around her and he wanted to scold her and shake her and tell her how foolish she'd been. "That was dangerous, Lucy. Promise me you'll never do anything like that again. The next time, you find a motel or you stay put."

She lifted her head. "I promise. Were you really worried?"

"As much as your family, maybe more. They had this mistaken idea that you had good sense. I thought about coming after you."

"Why?" she asked curiously.

"Just because," he murmured, taking the mug from her hand and setting it on the coffee table beside his. Then he gathered her closer to him and held her tight, letting his heat penetrate her sweatshirt.

They sat there for what seemed like an eternity

aware of each other's breathing, listening to the crackle of the logs in the fireplace, just cuddling close. Lucy's shivers dwindled away and he rubbed his cheek against hers feeling that it was finally warm.

"I couldn't stand the thought of something happening to you," he murmured.

"Nothing's going to happen to me, Zack." Her eyes carried a wealth of tenderness, so much that he almost turned away from it.

"Can I ask you something?" she asked in a low voice.

He shrugged and gave her a small smile. "Nothing's stopped you before."

"This might be a little awkward."

He leaned away. "What is it?"

"Were you attracted to Cassie?"

So it wasn't only the tension between them that had been bothering her. "No, I'm not attracted to Cassie."

"When I came into the kitchen before we left, I felt as if I were interrupting something."

"We were talking," he said. "That's all."

Lucy searched his face. "She looks just like me."

"On the surface maybe, but there are lots of differences."

"Like?" she pressed.

"Like the color of your hair. And when you smile, you have a dimple, she doesn't. You talk a little slower and you always smell like flowers. Cassie just smells clean." He smiled at her.

"She's a little curvier than I am," Lucy admitted.

Zack's brows arched. "I hadn't noticed."

"You're so diplomatic," she accused with laughter in her tone.

"I like you just the way you are," he assured her.

"Oh, Zack," she sighed looking up at him with such longing. He pulled her onto his lap, cover and all, and cradled her.

"You're getting under my skin, Lucy McIntyre, and I don't like it. But I can't seem to help wanting to do—" His lips brushed back and forth over hers teasingly. The afghan slid to the floor.

Zack couldn't control the need that ripped through him. His soft brushing of lips became nibbling and complete possession. He needed everything about Lucy. His tongue thrust into her mouth searching, asking, taking. Her fervent response made his arousal rage.

She only hesitated a moment before her fingers went to the buttons on his shirt and she undid them slowly, one by one. Then she slid her hand inside, letting her fingers sift through the soft hair.

His mouth covered Lucy's in a branding kiss that took all her breath. But she didn't care. Breathing wasn't nearly as important as kissing…kissing Zack. She lay against the pillow on the sofa's arm, and he stretched out on top of her. The weight of him was erotic. He was kissing her as if he'd never have another chance. She slid her arms around his back, wanting everything he could give her.

"Do you know how much I want you?" he growled.

"I want you, too," she murmured, "and we don't need protection. We can—"

All of a sudden, his expression changed and she felt his body tense.

Immediately one thought came to mind. She never should have reminded him that she wasn't a whole woman, that something was wrong with her.

"It does make a difference, doesn't it?" she asked hoarsely.

His brows arched. "*What* makes a difference?"

"That I can't have children."

He looked chagrinned. "Oh, Lucy, that has nothing to do with why I stopped. Believe me. I stopped because you're a virgin, we're in your parent's living room, and they're right upstairs. What if Marty should decide he wants a nightcap? Then there's the fact that I feel like I'm taking advantage of you after what you've been through tonight."

Her shame vanished. "I hiked through a snowstorm. I haven't been through a war."

The wry note in her voice made him smile. "Would this have happened if you didn't need to get warm?"

"It might have."

Pushing himself up, he sat a few inches from her, his hand raking through his hair. "I want you to be sure, Lucy. You've already told me what having sex means to you. And you know I'm not in a situation that I can make a commitment. This shouldn't be an impulsive decision for either of us."

Lucy knew she hadn't been acting out of impulse, but rather love. She loved Zackary Burke. But she knew he wasn't ready to hear it. If she said it, he might leave tomorrow. Maybe he was the one who needed time to come to terms with what was between them. Because if and when they slept together, they wouldn't be having sex, they'd be making love.

He straightened her sweatshirt and rebuttoned his, desire still obvious in his eyes. She combed her fingers through her hair, then raised her knees and wrapped her arms around them. "What now?" she asked him.

"Now it's time for bed."

"Zack…"

"I don't know, Lucy. When the time's right, we'll know it's right. *If* it's meant to be." Then he studied her closely. "Are you sure you're all right?"

"From the snowstorm, or from what just happened here?"

"Both."

"I'm a lot stronger than I look."

At that, he had to smile. "You're one of the strongest women I've ever met, and after talking to Cassie this weekend, she's a close second."

Still wondering what Cassie and Zack had talked about, Lucy didn't ask. If it was private, it was private and she knew Zack wouldn't betray a confidence. But why hadn't Cassie confided in her?

Swinging her legs from the sofa, Lucy picked up the mug of chocolate. Now it was only slightly warm. "Do you want more?" she asked.

Zack shook his head. "I'm going to turn in. With the snow tomorrow, there'll be a lot to do."

"I don't know if you'll be able to get my car out. We might have to wait till spring thaw."

Zack laughed. "I don't think it'll be that long. Was your trip successful?"

"Pretty much. I'm helping Mary Jo and Rick find Josh a used bike. A man in Long Brush said he might have a few next week. That's one of the reasons I drove to Chester. I didn't want to wait. But I didn't find anything there, either."

"After Rick gets back next week, maybe we could go into town together," he suggested. "If I'm going to be here for Christmas, I'd like to find something special for your Mom."

"*Are* you going to be here until Christmas?" she asked.

He hesitated a few moments, then answered her. "Yes."

She wondered when he'd made the decision and if it had anything to do with her. Rising to her feet, she leaned down and kissed him on the cheek. "You're a good man, Zack. And I like you a lot. It'll be great having you here for Christmas." She wanted to say so much more, but she didn't dare.

Before she took a risk that might bring disaster, she picked up his mug, too, and took them to the sink in the kitchen.

"Good night, Lucy," he said in a husky voice.

"Good night, Zack." When she'd finished rinsing the cups, he'd gone to his room. She leaned against the sink wanting his arms around her again, wanting to make love with him.

It would happen if it was meant to be.

Chapter Twelve

Sitting in a pew in the old country church beside Esther, Zack wondered what in the world he was doing here. He could have found plenty to keep him occupied at the ranch with Rick gone. The reverend in the pulpit was talking about faith and Christmas and Zack had turned him off. Last evening after supper, Lucy had invited him to come along. He'd agreed just to be with her. But as soon as they'd arrived, she'd been pressed into other service. Apparently the Sunday school teacher for the six-year-olds had gotten sick at the last minute and the pastor wanted Lucy to take over the class. She'd agreed and was downstairs in one of the basement rooms.

Zack glanced down the row beside him. Marty and Mary Jo sat with Tom and Esther listening intently to the man in the pulpit. Josh was downstairs in a class of his own. Even Marty seemed to be listening intently, but Zack felt he couldn't stay a moment longer.

Leaning close to Esther, he murmured, "I'm going to see how Lucy's faring."

Esther gave him a long look and then nodded. Sometimes he felt as if she could see into his soul, just like Lucy. It was unsettling. This whole service had been unsettling with it's evergreen boughs and Advent wreath and talk of light and love.

Out in the vestibule, Zack peered through one of the windows outside where the bright sun made the snow blinding. Zack marveled at all the cars in the parking lot. Church had never played much of a part in his life, but it seemed to for the McIntyre family.

Not understanding why, he looked back into the church at the people listening attentively. For some reason, he suddenly remembered all the feelings that had overcome him as he'd stood on the porch in the sleet and snow at Twin Pines Ranch. As Lucy had held him, he hadn't been able to contain the grief that he'd smothered for the past two years. Now it came rushing back again in a wave, and he almost wished he was sitting inside the church once more. But that would be foolish. He wasn't sure how long he stood there but finally he sucked in a deep breath and went down the stairs leading to the Sunday school rooms.

The doors were closed but he could see through the glass windows. When he caught sight of Lucy, he stopped. She was dressed in khakis with an ivory blouse and a vest embroidered with horses. She was sitting at the head of the circle with about ten children who were listening to her raptly. When one of them interrupted her, she looked up and saw him standing at the door. She beckoned to him to come inside.

When he opened the door, the children's heads

swung toward him. "Did you come to join us?" she asked.

"I thought I'd listen in." He took a chair outside of the circle, but in spite of that, Lucy said to the children, "This is Mr. Burke. He's a friend of mine."

The children seemed to accept that and they turned back to Lucy. Zack listened to the discussion as Lucy spoke to the six-year-olds about good deeds and preparing for Christmas. He watched her eyes when the children talked. He saw her joy at being with them. But something else, too. He suspected it was her longing to have children of her own, yet her knowledge that she never could. She'd be a terrific mom.

Zack's thoughts were interrupted when a little boy chimed up, "Mommy says I have to be nice to my sister or Santa won't come. Must I?"

Lucy smiled at him. "Maybe you should look at it another way. This isn't just a time to get ready for Christmas. We can start things now that we want to keep on doing to make ourselves and everyone around us happier. Wouldn't you like it if your sister was nice to you all the time?"

After a thoughtful pause, the little boy said, "I guess so."

"And maybe she'd like you to be nice to her all the time, too. And if you both are, wouldn't you be happier?"

"Who's going to tell her to be nice to *me*?" he wanted to know.

Lucy's smile grew broader. "Maybe no one has to tell her. If you start being nice to her, maybe she'll just naturally be nice back. It's worth a try, don't you think?"

He seemed to consider what she said, then gave her a shrug. The discussion turned to brothers and sisters and what they did and didn't do and Zack watched Lucy field their questions and answer them with sure confidence that she knew what she was talking about. She was grounded in her faith and her values and Zack envied her.

The time seemed to fly by as Zack listened and it didn't seem very long until Lucy ended the class, asking them all to draw a picture for next week of one special thing they were going to try to do for Advent.

As they scurried out the door to meet their parents, Zack went over to the desk where Lucy was picking up her coat from the chair. "You're very good with them."

"I love children."

"But it hurts you to be around them, doesn't it?"

She shrugged. "It hurts more not to be."

Along with other thoughts he'd tried to keep locked in a box, he remembered how he'd loved his work being a doctor. He'd liked listening to his patients and helping them. But after Kay and their child died, he'd been filled with a feeling of powerlessness. His work had reminded him that he'd failed to help the most important person in his life. He'd not only felt like a failure as a doctor, but as a husband, too.

For a brief moment, he'd considered telling Lucy about being a doctor, but as she put her coat on, he dismissed the idea. If he told her, she'd try to convince him to practice again. He was sure of it. He wasn't ready for that, and he didn't know if he ever would be. So it was better just to keep that part of his past hidden.

Outside, Zack took Lucy's arm as they walked to the truck.

"Uh oh," she said under her breath.

"What?"

There were two young women standing at a car ahead of them. Lucy explained, "The blonde is Angie Devane. She was Marty's girlfriend. I don't think he's seen her since they broke up."

When Zack scanned the parking lot, he saw Marty stop at the edge of it looking directly at the woman Lucy had mentioned. There was such a look of anguish on his face that Zack wished he could offer him some reassurance that he could go on without her, that the memories would eventually heal. But Zack wasn't so sure of that himself.

Marty looked away from the women and quickly climbed inside his father's 4x4, slamming the door hard behind him.

"I wish I could do more for him," Lucy said.

"You're doing all you can, Lucy. He has to do the rest." Zack opened her car door for her and she climbed inside. When he closed the door, Zack's words echoed in his head and he wondered what he needed to do to heal the past.

Maybe he and Marty were in the same boat after all.

Throughout Sunday dinner, Lucy watched Zack. He was more restless than usual, quiet again. He couldn't safely take his Harley out on the snow-dotted roads and she imagined he might be feeling hemmed in. Before she said anything to Zack she went to her father to tell him she wanted to use their snowmobiles.

Zack had gone outside and she went to find him. When she did, he was feeding Blazer an apple.

"He's doing really well," she said, coming up to Zack. "I'm going to start riding him this week."

"Are you sure he'll let you?"

"He'll let me. We've become friends." As she let the silence stretch between, she thought about what had happened on the sofa the other night.

"I have a surprise for you," she said.

"What kind of surprise?"

"Come with me and I'll show you. We have to go to that small garage over at Rick's."

Narrowing his gaze, he studied her, but he didn't ask any more questions. "All right."

They walked up the road side by side, the sun shining brightly before them. The countryside still looked clean and pure and bright. The pines were still laden with snow and icicles formed on the eaves of buildings. Their breaths puffed out in front of them as they walked, and Lucy led Zack to an outbuilding next to Rick's garage. Taking off one glove she worked the combination lock, then flipped it open. Zack noticed the snowmobiles immediately.

"What have we got here?"

"Something a little more streamlined than a horse. How would you like to take them out?"

He chuckled. "I shouldn't be surprised that you can drive one of these things."

"Rick and Dad use them for fun, but they can also get to the cattle quickly if they have to in really deep snows. Are you game?"

His grin was contagious. "You bet I am. It'll be as good as being on my bike again."

That's exactly how she thought he'd see it. It wasn't long before they'd strapped helmets on their heads and settled on the snowmobiles.

"Where shall we go?" he asked her.

She pointed to the west. "Let's head in that direction. There's something I want to show you."

Lucy watched as Zack got the feel for the machine and became comfortable with it. They rode side by side over the snow enjoying the speed and the air and the scenery. The sky was winter blue and cloudless. Being out here was like breaking a frontier. There were no footprints, no truck tracks, no sign of anything human for miles. It was an isolating feeling yet also an invigorating one.

They'd traveled miles from the house when Lucy pointed ahead to a building in the distance. Pines flanked its north side. They took the snowmobiles almost up to the door. After they switched off the ignitions, Zack took off his helmet and so did she.

"What have we got here?" he asked, a serious look in his eyes.

"I come here when I want to get away from everyone and everything...when I want to think. I suspect Marty's been spending a lot of time here lately. There's a small fireplace inside. I don't know if there's any firewood though."

"I suppose we could warm up before we go back," Zack said matter-of-factly.

"That's what I thought." Tucking her helmet under her arm, she went to the door and opened it. Zack followed her inside.

Lucy looked around trying to see it through Zack's eyes. There was a single cot made up like a bed with a patchwork quilt. The one chair that sat before the fireplace looked as if it had seen years of wear. The green cushions were lumpy but comfortable. Lucy had spent a lot of time in that chair. There was a stack of magazines and another of books. A five-gallon water container sat near the cot with paper cups. The brick fireplace was cone-shaped with a small flat hearth. There was a storage box for kindling and a few logs beside it.

Zack peered into the grate. "Looks as if it's been used recently." He went to pick up something beside the chair and held it up for her to see. It was a liquor bottle and it was empty.

She shook her head. "We leave him alone when he comes up here. Maybe we shouldn't."

"He'd only go somewhere else if you came after him," Zack said sagely. Spotting a metal box propped on the hearth, he guessed what was inside. "Looks as if we have everything we need for a fire. Should I get it started?"

"That would be great. I wish I had thought to bring Thermoses of coffee or hot chocolate. All we've got is water and…" She took something out of her coat pocket. "A candy bar. I'll split it with you," she said with a smile.

"That sounds like an offer I can't refuse."

It didn't take long until Zack had the fire burning brightly. Flames leapt toward the chimney and heat soon filled the small room. Shedding her coat and gloves, Lucy laid them on the stack of magazines and sat on the cot. After Zack brushed off his hands, he took off his jacket and came to sit beside her. After church he'd changed into jeans and a heavy blue sweater. She'd pulled out a Christmas sweatshirt decorated with a snowman.

Breaking the candy bar in half, she offered him a piece. "Chocolate with almonds. My favorite."

He laughed. "I'll have to remember that when I Christmas shop for you."

"You don't have to get me anything." She'd been working every spare moment she had on a wooden stallion she wanted to give him for Christmas.

"It's not a matter of 'having to'," he commented.

As Lucy took a bite of her chocolate, her gaze met Zack's.

"Why did you bring me here, Lucy?" he asked.

"I thought you were restless and wanted to get out for a bit."

"But why did you bring me here?"

The heat from the fire was warming her, but she knew it wasn't the flames on the hearth that caused the heat in her body. "I thought it might be nice to spend a little bit of time alone."

Taking her chin in his palm, he lifted it to him. "Why?"

Her mouth went dry, but she managed, "To talk."

He shook his head. "I don't think so. We can talk anywhere."

Suddenly embarrassed by what she was thinking, maybe by the unconscious motive that had suggested their trip here, she started to move away from him. "We don't have to stay. I just thought—"

Catching her arm, he kept her from rising. "I won't ask you exactly what you thought, but tell me, does it have something to do with this?"

His lips on hers were seductive and coaxing and teasing, all at the same time. She knew she'd come here for this…to be alone with Zack…to make love with him. She was ready to accept loving him for the moment, rather than not loving him at all. Maybe she could convince him love was worth taking a risk for…maybe she could convince herself.

Zack's tongue traced her lips and she trembled from the sheer erotic pleasure of it. She reached around Zack and when he dipped inside her mouth, she grabbed hold of his sweater to steady herself.

While she was still dizzy from his kiss, he pulled back and gazed at her. "We could get more comfortable."

She nodded.

"Let's move the mattress and covers in front of the fire," he suggested.

After Zack lifted the cot's mattress to the floor, he layered it with the covers, mindful of what they were about to do.

"You can still change your mind," he assured her, standing over the makeshift bed.

She shook her head.

His expression was serious as he took her hand and drew her toward him. Against his chest, she laid her head on his shoulder as he wrapped his arms around her and held her close. The crackling of the fire was the only sound in the room as their hearts synchronized, beating at the same tempo, faster and harder. When she lifted her face to him, he ran his thumb caressingly over her lips.

She shivered as the pleasure caught fire everywhere in her body. Catching his thumb with her lips, she laved the tip with her tongue. Desire flared brighter in his eyes and he brought his lips to hers. His kiss was slow and unhurried, stoking their desire, making her anticipate everything that was to come. His hands went to the band of her sweatshirt and he tucked it up, stroking the soft skin underneath. His fingers were long and hot and slightly calloused. As they passed over her sides, up toward her bra, she moaned softly.

He pulled her sweatshirt up and over her head, then brushed her bra straps over her shoulders. Her bra fell away onto the floor on top of the sweatshirt. Then he pulled his own sweater over his head and his hands went to the snap on his jeans.

Lucy went still, not sure what to do next, worrying about how she could pleasure him. She didn't know the first thing about making love with a man.

As if he sensed her thoughts, he said, "Let's take off our boots. The rest will be easier."

And the rest was. He helped her slide out of her jeans and then discarded his. Lying naked in front of the fire, he covered her with the quilt.

"You're beautiful in the firelight," he said, pushing her hair behind her ear, then stroking through the waves.

"Zack, I don't know what to do. Tell me what to do."

Stretching on his side, he urged her to do the same. He stroked her cheek with his hand and kissed it, then her chin, then her eyelids. Each one of his soft kisses made her restless for much more. Reaching out to him, she slid her hand over his shoulder, down his arm. After she touched his chest hair again, she played in it, making small designs, watching the pleasure on his face. He was aroused, and before she even considered what she was about to do, her hand passed down his stomach, over his navel, and curled around him.

"Lucy," he said with a gasp.

She caressed him and he closed his eyes, accepting her gift. But then he caught her wrist. "It's your turn," he said in a deep husky voice.

He kissed down her throat to her breasts, laved the nipple, explored the underside as she made soft sounds with the pleasure of it. While his tongue teased one nipple, his hand slid over her waist, down her hip, and caressed her thigh. As his fingers moved between her legs, she clasped his shoulder.

"Easy, Lucy," he murmured. "Just relax and go with it."

Relax, when he was making every nerve in her body dance? Relax, when she wanted his hands all over her body? How could she relax?

His fingers expertly stroked her and took her on the most exciting journey she'd ever experienced.

"Zack," she cried, as a wave of pleasure started building.

"Go with it," he said again and kissed her.

She felt as if she were climbing higher and higher toward an unknown summit. As his tongue stroked her mouth, his fingers brought her to a fever pitch of need.

"Zack, I want you."

Rolling her to her back, he rose above her. "I want you too, Lucy, like I've never wanted anyone."

Zack's kiss became even more passionate as he tantalized her with pleasure but still didn't enter her.

Instinctively she lifted her knees. "Please, Zack," she whispered, as he broke the kiss to take in air.

"Lucy, this might not be all pleasure…"

Arching toward him, she blurted out, "I don't care. I want you. Now."

He entered her with maddening slowness and kissed her with almost desperate desire. She felt her body tighten around him. Then as he moved, a glorious sensation began. It lifted her higher and higher, faster and faster, until only Zack existed. His thrusts became more forceful and she met them, eager to give him as much pleasure as he was giving her. She felt his skin glisten. Hers did, too, as they both frantically sought release. It came as a shattering explosion, rocking them both simultaneously. She held onto Zack, afraid to let go, afraid she was dreaming, afraid their union would end.

It did end.

He was still for many heartbeats. But then he rolled to his side, leaving her feeling empty. She could sense a change in him and she had to know why.

"Zack?" she asked.

Staring up at the ceiling, he didn't answer her right away.

Zack didn't know what he was going to say to Lucy. He'd expected to find physical satisfaction, not an earth-shattering experience that whirled his thoughts and emotions into turmoil. And the look in Lucy's eyes as he'd given her the ultimate pleasure…

He'd made a mistake by giving into his desire for her and now he didn't know what to do about it. The last thing in the world he wanted to do was hurt her.

"We never should have come here, Lucy."

"Why not?"

He could hear the slight quaver in her voice. "As soon as we walked in here, I should have turned around and walked out again."

"Why didn't you?"

"Because I thought we could enjoy the moment without this getting complicated. But I was stupid to think that."

"You asked me if this is what I wanted and I said it was."

He faced her, knowing he had to make her see this situation for what it was. "And what now, Lucy? What do you expect to happen? Do you expect me to stay because we slept together? Do you expect me to feel responsibility because you'd never been with a man before?"

"No!" She sat up looking hurt and angry. "You don't have any responsibility toward me, Zack. I knew exactly what I was doing. I know that you intend to leave. You made that perfectly clear."

Sitting up too, he caught her arm. "You're the type of woman who deserves promises. Don't you understand that?"

"Maybe I do deserve promises, maybe I don't. But I didn't ask for any." Scrambling to her feet, she started dressing. "We'd better get back. It's getting dark and I don't want my family to worry again."

He heard the unsteadiness of her words underneath her bravado, and he wanted to put his arms around her and pull her down to the mattress again. But he didn't. She not only deserved promises, she deserved a hell of a lot more than he could give her. She definitely didn't need a man who didn't know where he'd be tomorrow.

They straightened up the cabin in silence. While Lucy folded the covers, Zack doused the fire. He just wished he could douse the fire inside of him as easily.

Dusk was indeed falling as they put on their helmets and mounted the snowmobiles. Without another word, Lucy started hers up and zoomed off ahead of him. He drew up beside her thinking about what a mess he'd made of everything.

At Rick's shed, Zack pushed the snowmobiles inside and Lucy locked the door. As they walked toward her home, her steps were quick and fast as if she couldn't wait to get away from him.

At the porch, he couldn't stand the silence between them a moment longer. "Lucy, if you want me to leave, I will."

She stared at him in the dimming light, searching his face. Finally, she said, "If you can leave that easily, then maybe you should." With that, she climbed the porch steps and opened the door.

Zack knew he had a soul-searching decision to make…and soon.

Chapter Thirteen

Zack's decision to leave after Christmas weighed heavily on him as he exercised horses Wednesday afternoon, realizing how much he enjoyed having twelve-hundred pounds of intuitive animal under his saddle. These horses were well trained, in large part due to Lucy.

Lucy.

He couldn't stop thinking about her as he'd turned in at night. Hell, he couldn't stop thinking about her any time of the day, either. Making love with her was a vivid DVD in his mind. But almost just as vivid was her hug on her sister's porch when he'd finally let his grief free. He'd been embarrassed and hadn't wanted her to see his emotion. But emotion churned inside of him all the time now. That hadn't been true before he'd arrived at the Rising Star. That hadn't been true since his wife died.

As a physician, he was used to compartmentalizing, though after Kay had died he'd slipped into physician mode twenty-four hours a day. Only, nothing about his work had been satisfying. It had made him forget, at least while he was caring for a patient. But working those long hours wasn't living and maybe he'd gone on the road to learn how to live again.

Returning to L.A. and some kind of practice seemed to be the logical choice. But he wasn't feeling logical these days.

Christmas was a big deal on the Rising Star. There were evergreen wreaths with red bows everywhere. Lucy and her mom and Mary Jo had hung them over the past few days. They'd also been baking cookies and getting ready for the annual Christmas open house this coming weekend. Lucy's mom had invited him, of course, and he didn't feel as if he could turn her down. Yet he didn't know how he was going to handle all that holiday cheer. He remembered Thanksgiving and how he'd felt sitting around the table with the McIntyres…how he'd been grateful he was there.

Dismounting, he handed off the bay to one of the hands. "Do you want me to unsaddle and groom her?"

He usually did it himself. It was all part of the work on the Rising Star.

But Hank shook his head. "No need. I'll do it. But Rick and Tom are in the mares' barn, making sure the inoculation reports are up to date. And I thought I saw Miss Lucy trying to shore up a fence post in the barn's main corral. She probably could use some help with that."

Rick had just returned yesterday and was trying to catch up with what he'd missed. "I'm glad you told me. I'll give her a hand."

He'd tried to stay away from Lucy since their trip to the cabin. He'd thought that was the best thing to do. But when he spotted her in the corral, his gut churned and all he wanted to do was wrap his arms around her, haul her inside and make love to her again.

Pulling in a long breath, he gazed up the lane at Mary Jo and Rick's house. Two horses were tethered to the split rail fence that bordered the front yard. That wasn't unusual to see and the site made Zack smile. Here, riding a horse was almost as easy as jumping on his bike to get from point A to point B.

Next his line of site rested on the McIntyres' family home—the home where Lucy had grown up. There was so much warmth and caring in that house that Zack knew it spilled out onto everyone the family encountered. Tonight Tom would light the lights he'd attached to the porch roof and railing, signaling that Christmas was indeed on its way.

Focusing on Lucy again, he strode toward her.

She looked up when she heard his bootfalls on the gravel. Her smile was slow in coming, but it did come, and as always it packed a wallop.

"Need a hand?" Zack asked nonchalantly—or at least he hoped he was nonchalant—as he came up beside her. Gazing down at her, his chest tightened.

"I'm almost finished," she said, placing the hammer on the top fence rung, her voice sounding a little trembly.

Because they were standing so close? Or because she wanted him to leave and was too polite to say so?

He looked over the job she'd done. "It looks good. *You* look good."

She was wearing a short purple wool coat that she often wore to work in, but her hair was long and free. He slid his hand under her hair to the nape of her neck. She was gazing up at him with a mixture of wariness and disappointment, and maybe a little bit of hope. That expression in her eyes made his throat tighten.

He was trying to find some words when suddenly Josh came running down the lane. Seeing them, he veered toward them. He wasn't wearing a coat, and he looked windblown and panicked. "Our house is on fire! Come help, come help!"

Zack didn't hesitate for a second and neither did Lucy, as they ran after her nephew at full speed. "Isn't Mary Jo there?" Zack asked as they ran.

"She's with Mom, baking. Marty was supposed to take Josh for a ride after school then watch him."

As they ran, Lucy asked her nephew, "What happened, honey?"

Josh was crying as he managed to say, "When we got back from riding, Marty had a bottle in his pocket. He drank it. Then he couldn't stand up straight! He tried to take the hot chocolate off the stove but the potholder caught fire. Then the napkins caught fire!"

Zack saw Lucy's expression and understood her guilt.

"I should have stopped him," she said. "I should have made him get help. What if something had happened to Josh?"

"He's fine," Zack assured her. "He's fine." But where was Marty?

Zack reached the house first and saw smoke billowing out the door. He didn't think twice about rushing into the house to find Marty.

Zack assessed the flames, flipped the charred potholder into the sink, turned on the water full force, grabbed the sprayer and began drenching the fire. It had caught the quilted mixer cover, the paper towel roll under the upper cupboard and the cupboards themselves.

Zack saw Marty standing like a statue near the living room, coughing, looking panicked.

When Lucy rushed in, she saw what Zack was doing. After she grabbed an afghan from the sofa, Zack watered it down then took the cover and batted the flames.

Five minutes later, they had doused the fire.

The place was a mess when they'd finished. Eyes burning from the smoke, the taste of soot in his mouth, Zack stood beside Lucy studying the kitchen. The cupboards would have to be refinished. The backsplash behind the sink had melted. As Zack was making sure all of the fire was out, Lucy crossed to Marty and shook his arm.

Zack heard Lucy say, "You need help and I won't cover for you ever again."

"I don't need help," Marty yelled at her. "I need to be left alone!" Zack was too busy assessing the damage to care about Marty.

In a rush, Mary Jo came running in with Josh in tow. "I saw you running up here and—" She held her hand over her mouth in astonishment and then started to cry. Huffing and puffing, Tom and Esther burst inside, too. Lucy's mom held Mary Jo, while Tom comforted Josh, telling him it could all be fixed.

But then Rick came barreling in, looked around, then cast his focus on Marty. "I trusted you to watch my son." Standing close to him, he said, "You wreak of alcohol. You need professional help."

"Don't think I'm going to one of those places where they tell me something to do every hour of the day," Marty shouted. "I *won't* do it. You all think you're so superior. You all have a crutch of some kind. Mom's and Lucy's are kind of the same. They care for everybody all the time. That's their crutch for getting through life. You, you're good at math and lumber. You build things. That's your crutch. And Dad— His horses are his crutch. He knows they need him to make their lives better. He trains them the best he can, so they're ready for a new owner. But they're his crutch for when he doesn't know what to do next, for when he gets in a tiff with Mom, for when he doesn't know what to say to us. He goes to the horses. Me? I'm not good at anything. Sure, I take care of the horses, but not like you all do. With me, it's something to do. With all of you, it's something that pours from your fingers onto their coats. It's something that connects you to them. Even Zack. It's the horses that brought him here and I can see why. They relate to him like a puppy to a master. I used to have Angie. She was my crutch. Now I don't. So now I have something else. And just because none of you approve of it doesn't mean it's not the right thing for me." He started for the door.

Lucy called after him, "You can't leave like this. You can't even walk straight. You were supposed to be taking care of Josh. How could you do that knowing you didn't have your full senses? Do you realize what could have happened here? How we could have lost Josh *and* you?"

Although unsteady, Marty stopped in the doorway. "You're over-dramatizing. You always do. We'll get a cleanup crew in here for the kitchen. It will be fine."

"But you won't be fine," Lucy insisted. "Do you think Mary Jo is ever going to leave you with Josh again? Do you think I'm ever going to let you go riding without someone else with you? Do you think I'd even trust you to drive Mom to church? Marty, realize what you did here today. Some of this is my fault because I didn't tell what was going on. When you came home drunk, I should have told Mom and Dad. Maybe they could have gotten through to you before this happened. Mary Jo's beautiful kitchen is ruined. But worse than that, our trust in you is ruined."

"You're wrong," Marty snapped, still slurring his words. "Nuthin's ruined. I wouldn't have hurt Josh."

"What if that fire had gotten out of hand and had crossed to the door and had the two of you trapped in here. What would you have done? Could you have even thought straight enough to *think* about what you would have done?"

Zack had never seen Lucy so angry, never seen her trying so hard to get a point across. But Marty was in complete denial and wasn't buying any of it.

He ran out of the house to where he'd hitched the horses. After he managed to get his foot in the stirrup, he launched himself up onto Alfredo. Then he took off down the lane.

Zack stepped out onto the porch. He saw Marty head toward the side field. But there were snow banks blocking access.

Lucy ran out and saw what Marty was going to do before anyone else. "No, Marty! Don't try to jump them. Not with Alfredo. He doesn't like those wide jumps," she shouted.

But by then, Marty wasn't listening at all.

Zack could see the disaster about to happen. He could see a bad situation in the making. He climbed on the other horse at the rail and galloped after Lucy's brother.

All of it seemed to happen in slow motion. At the snow bank, Alfredo balked. When Marty still urged him forward, Alfredo rose up on his back legs and pawed at the air. Then his hooves slammed down hard on the ground, jarring Marty. Once more, he rose up and twisted.

In that twist Marty fell off and hit hard against the fence.

Zack didn't like the looks of the way he'd fallen. He didn't like the looks of Marty's stillness as he lay there.

He raced his horse to Marty, reined him in and jumped off. By the time he reached Lucy's brother, he suspected Marty wasn't breathing. There was a angry-looking red brush burn across his throat! From the trauma of hitting the fence post, his airway was obstructed. Zack knew he had to do something fast. But he had to be sure what came next. With a doctor's eyes and ears and intuition, Zack quickly examined Lucy's brother and diagnosed the problem. It wasn't just that Marty wasn't breathing. He wasn't *able* to breathe. There were no gasping sounds, no coughing.

Lucy had run up the lane after Zack. He yelled to her, "Call the paramedics."

Zack performed the Heimlich maneuver without dislodging anything. He heard Lucy as she spoke into her phone but he knew they couldn't wait. Marty needed oxygen and he needed it now.

Patting his pocket, Zack found his pocket knife. He'd always kept it shiny and honed because it was a keepsake he cherished. Now that keepsake had to save Marty's life. If he screwed this up—

Zack couldn't think about that.

Lucy was staring at him with wide, frightened eyes. "What are you doing?"

"He can't breathe. I need to perform an emergency tracheotomy. Don't watch, okay?"

"Zack!"

"He'll die if he doesn't soon get some air."

Taking a ball point pen from his pocket, he unscrewed the lid and dumped out the inside. He ran the tube through the snow, but he knew infection was the least of his problems at this point. Slipping into professional doctor mode, as if it was a habit he couldn't forget, he found the indentation between Marty's Adam's apple and the cricoid cartilage. Then he took a deep breath and made a half-inch horizontal incision, about one-half-inch deep.

He heard Lucy's gasp. He heard her say, "Oh, Zack," with tears in her voice.

But he couldn't be distracted by her. Not now. After he pinched the incision, he slid his finger inside the slit to open it. Once he'd inserted the tube of the pen into the incision, he breathed into it with two quick breaths. He paused five seconds, then gave one breath every five seconds. Finally he saw Marty's chest rise, and his eyes fluttered open. He was getting the air he needed.

Quickly Zack placed a hand on Marty's shoulder. "Easy, real easy. You *can* breathe, it's just not the same as usual. Take it slow and easy. Help's on its way."

When Lucy dropped to the ground beside her brother, Zack could see she was putting together everything in her head, everything she'd learned about him, everything she'd seen him do. And suddenly, with the flash of insight on her face, he saw that she realized he was a *doctor*. Immediately after, an emotion moistened her eyes—one that he'd seen there before. Hurt. She was hurt that he'd kept a secret like this from her…hurt because he hadn't confided in her. Because he hadn't, she must believe she wasn't important to him.

Looking away, she brushed Marty's hair back and whispered, "Everything's going to be all right."

Zack wanted to believe that. Her brother had to go into rehab and Zack would do everything in his power to make that happen. But as far as the two of them—

Zack switched off the thoughts that crowded in and watched Marty carefully as they waited for the ambulance. He concentrated on his patient, heartsick he hadn't told Lucy the entire truth about his life, aching because there was so much he needed to say to her. But now wasn't the time to say it.

When the paramedics arrived, Zack flipped credentials out of his wallet, credentials the McIntyre family had never seen. All of them seemed to be in shock. None of them seemed to know what to say. They were all concerned about Marty and they weren't asking questions. Mary Jo had taken Josh to her mom's house so he wouldn't be scared. Soon, Zack hoped, he'd have the opportunity to explain it all to the little boy in terms a five-year-old could understand.

Because of his ID, the EMT personnel agreed to let Zack ride with Marty in the ambulance to the hospital. No one protested.

Before he climbed in the back, Lucy murmured, "You know what's best for him."

She sounded so sad, as if she'd done something terribly wrong. *Everyone* had had a part to play in this—in enabling Marty, in denying what was really happening. He'd have to reassure her of that later and hope that her guilt would abate. The whole McIntyre family had just wanted Marty's problems to go away. That was typical.

Still, Zack hated leaving Lucy there…hated seeing the disappointment in her eyes right before the ambulance pulled away.

At the hospital Marty was taken directly to the O.R. so a proper procedure could be performed. Lucy, Tom and Esther, and Rick had to go through the paperwork nightmare of having Marty admitted. While they did, Zack paced, walked up and down halls, made a few calls and remembered when a hospital had been part of his daily routine. Today had opened his eyes to how much he missed practicing medicine. He'd also been reminded of how a crisis could change *everything*.

When Kay and his unborn son had died, he'd felt as if he'd lost his life overnight. He'd not only lost his family but his future. Fate was fickle. Marty could have died if Zack hadn't been there and known what to do. The McIntyres' lives could have been changed forever with Marty's fall from his horse and the trauma of banging his throat on that fencepost. Life could turn on a dime or in an instant. Or…

It could turn in the meeting of two minds and hearts and souls when a couple made love. The day he'd made love to Lucy, his whole world had been shaken in a different way than before, and he hadn't known how to handle it. He hadn't known how to change his loner lifestyle…how to hope for a future…how to finally let his grief out and push it behind him.

Yet Lucy had helped him start to leave the past behind. She truly was his light, and he had to tell her that. But he knew he couldn't tell her until they all knew that Marty would be okay.

To his chagrin, Lucy didn't come near him as they waited for Marty to come out of recovery. But she did glance at him often. Zack caught many of those glances. He tried to hold her gaze, but she wouldn't hold his. His heart was aching because he didn't know what she thought—of him, of the situation, of the two of them together. However, he was going to find out very soon.

They all entered Marty's room when he was awake

enough to have visitors. Zack wasn't surprised when Tom motioned him along in. Lucy's dad said, "You saved his life. You have to come in here with us."

Zack liked the feeling that Tom thought he belonged there, but neither Marty nor their family might like what he had to say.

Marty was hooked up to an IV and Zack knew Lucy's brother was being given antibiotics to fight infection. He had a bandage around the tube in the throat that could hopefully be removed in a few days. The air in the room was being humidified. The McIntyres crowded around Marty as he wrote on a pad that he was okay and they should stop worrying!

Zack crossed to his bedside and just stood there.

When Marty looked up at him, his eyes grew shiny.

Zack said, "I knew what I was doing. I'm a doctor of internal medicine. So I wasn't just experimenting on you."

Marty gave him a crooked smile, then held out his hand to thank him.

Zack shook Marty's hand, but then he asked, "You know what you have to do, don't you?"

Marty looked down at the sheet.

"Marty?" Zack asked in challenge.

Marty took the pad and pen again and wrote: *I do need help.*

Zack nodded. "Yes, you do. I've made some calls. I can get you into a rehab center in Sheridan as soon as you're released.

Marty took the pen and pad again: *Over Christmas?*

"Well, that's the thing," Zack admitted. "We'll have about two weeks before Christmas. If you do well, and you work on your issues during that time, the facility could give you a day pass as long as I watch over you. I'm sure your mom and dad and sister will agree to do anything they have to do to have you home for the holiday. No spiked egg nog and plenty of presents for all. What do you think?"

Closing his eyes for a moment, Marty thought about it, returned his gaze to his family and then nodded.

Zack had to be honest with Lucy's brother. "You know this isn't going to be easy."

Marty wrote: *It won't be as hard as today.*

Zack said to the McIntyres, "I can get you reading material on what you can do to help him. If we have everybody on the same page, you could get your old Marty back."

Without hesitation, Esther crossed to Zack, hugged him and gave him a kiss on the cheek. "Thank you."

"I didn't do anything except remember how to be a doctor. Now if you don't mind, Lucy and I have a few things to discuss."

Lucy's gaze snapped to his and he saw confusion there. He didn't want to see confusion. He wanted to see so much more.

He nodded for her to walk with him. She did, but in silence. When they reached a small waiting room, they stepped inside and Zack closed the door.

"Zack, what are you doing? Families wait in here while—"

"We need privacy. I can't just say I love you out in the hall."

Her eyes widened, her mouth rounded into an O.

Then she shook her head. "How can you expect me to believe you love me if you didn't trust me enough to tell me you were a *doctor*?"

Taking her by the hands, he pulled her toward him. "Look at me, Lucy, so that you know what I'm saying is the truth."

Her gaze didn't leave his.

"I knew if I told you I was a doctor, you'd try to convince me to practice again. So many of my friends and colleagues did that and it just made everything worse. I needed to forget I was a doctor for a while. I just needed to be...a man. And figure out what came next. Now I know what can come next if you'll agree."

After studying his face for what seemed like an eternity, a gentle smile broke across her lips and the confusion in her gaze transformed into something so radiant he almost couldn't believe what he was seeing.

Reaching up, she stroked his jaw. "Then you underestimated my love for you. Because I want you to be free to be whatever you want to be. After all, you're always going to be my cowboy."

"So you do love me?" he prompted, needing to hear her say it.

She wrapped her arms around his neck. "I love you, Zackary Burke, whether you're a cowboy, or a doctor, or a drifter, or anything in between. You've been in my heart for a while now, maybe since Thanksgiving Day when you took my hand and I knew you wanted to be sitting there with me."

"All I had to do was take your hand to win your heart?" he teased.

"Well, maybe those few kisses thrown in helped," she said a little coyly.

"Then holding you in my arms and kissing you right now should be a real blockbuster moment."

But as he bent his head, Lucy stopped him. "I have to ask you, Zack, does my inability to have children matter to you?"

Of course, she'd think of that. He just hoped she'd believe him when he assured her, "You matter to me."

"You really mean that, don't you?" Her voice was filled with wonder at the thought.

"I do," he said solemnly. "I want to live here and ranch along with practicing medicine. You're everything I've ever wanted in a wife and I want to build a family with you. We can adopt. There are so many kids who need loving parents. So just to make this official, Lucy McIntyre, will you marry me?"

She didn't hesitate a moment. "Oh, yes, Zack. I'll marry you! And I'll love you forever."

"A cowboy *or* a doctor can't ask for anymore than that."

As Zack kissed Lucy his world got shaken up all over again. But this time, he went along with the world's rocking sensations...because this time he gave into the happiness overtaking him, as well as the passion.

He gave into the idea that he'd found a true home.

Epilogue

Lucy gazed around the living room at her family, but not just her adopted family. Cassie had come to spend Christmas with them. Her twin had squealed over Lucy's engagement ring and given her a huge hug. Their glances met now and Lucy could see that Cassie was truly happy for her.

The scent of pine from the Christmas tree wafted through the room as Zack, who was sitting next to her, wrapped his arm around her.

Josh opened another present, revealing a giant set of Legos. He rushed over to Zack. "Thank you, thank you! They're almost as great as the bicycle Mom and Dad got me." Then he hugged Zack and Lucy, too.

In an armchair by the fireplace, Marty laughed. A genuine laugh.

Early this morning she and Zack had driven to Sheridan to pick him up to bring him home for Christmas dinner and their celebration. He'd lost weight but seemed happy and more peaceful than he'd been in a while. He and Zack had talked for a long time before dinner and Zack had given her a thumbs-up sign afterward. There was so much hope there.

So much hope for a bright future for them all. Lucy had exchanged gifts with Zack last evening. She had given him the stallion she'd carved for him. He'd given her a heart-shaped gold locket so she'd know his heart was always close to hers.

But now she plucked a box from under the tree and set it on his knee.

"What's this?"

"My present to you."

"But you already—"

She put a finger over his lips. "Open it."

He kissed her finger, his heated gaze warming her all over. Then he unwrapped the small box and opened the lid. There was a key lying inside.

When he removed it, he arched a brow. "I already have the key to your heart, so I can't imagine what this belongs to."

She laughed. "Look under the cotton."

He removed the cotton and took out a folded picture. She explained, "That's our apartment in town. It's an old Victorian and we have the first floor."

Zack's brows arched but he was smiling because privacy was hard to come by right now. "Are you sure you want to leave the ranch?"

"With you opening a practice in town, the apartment will be more convenient. We can move in right away or we can wait until we get married on Valentine's Day."

He pretended to think about it. "We could start getting it ready and spend some time there." He tilted his forehead against hers.

From the chair beside the sofa, her father said, "Oh, we'd be glad to help you get it ready."

Lucy saw the amused glint in her father's eye as he went on, "Eventually you'll have to build a house big enough for a family reunion. There's a lot of land here you could use to build on. One of those fancy SUVs could get you back and forth in good time for your office hours."

"Now there's a thought," Zack said. "After all, I wouldn't want Blazer to forget me. I'll need to ride for exercise and that would be convenient if we were living on the ranch."

"I'd love a house here," Lucy admitted. "But that's a big decision."

"And one we'll make together," Zack assured her.

Then, not caring that her whole family was watching, Lucy kissed Zack, promising him her heart and her life, eager to make vows that would last a lifetime.

KAREN ROSE SMITH BOOKS
AVAILABLE IN E-BOOK FORMAT

SEARCH FOR LOVE Series
*Nathan's Vow, Book 1 *
*Jake's Bride, Book 2 *
*Always Devoted, Book 3 *
*Always Her Cowboy, Book 4 *
Heartfire, Book 5
*Cassidy's Cowboy, Book 6 *
*Her Sister, Book 7 *

FOREVER LOVE Series
*April's Promise *

FINDING MR. RIGHT Series
Kit and Kisses, Book 1
Forever After, Book 2
*When Mom Meets Dad, Book 3 *
*Falling For Her Boss, Book 4 *
*Toys and Baby Wishes, Book 5 *
Love in Bloom, Book 6
*Ribbons and Rainbows, Book 7 *
*Wish on the Moon, Book 8 *
*A Man Worth Loving, Book 9 *

EVERYDAY LOVE Short Story Series
Everyday Cinderellas, Vol. 1
Everyday Prince Charming, Vol. 2
Everyday Romance, Vol.3

Garden of Fantasy
Abigail and Mistletoe
Writing is a Business

SCIENCE FICTION
SHORT STORY COLLECTION
Journey Into Chaos

BOXED SETS
Finding Mr. Right Box Set One
Finding Mr. Right Boxed Set Two
Search For Love Boxed Set One
Search For Love Boxed Set Two
Everyday Love Boxed Set

*Also available as an audio book

Excerpt from HER SISTER
Search For Love series, Book 7

Prologue

Where is Lynnie? Where did she go?

In her mind, five-year-old Clare Thaddeus called to her little sister—*Come back, Lynnie. Please come back.*

The huge policeman crouched down in front of Clare's mother at the sofa and said in a deep, slow voice, "Mrs. Thaddeus, I know you're terribly upset. But I need details. We've got an hour before daylight. If your daughter wandered outside—"

Clare's father, who'd been talking to another man in blue, glanced at her, and Clare huddled down deeper into the big green armchair. Her dad didn't come to her but rather went to her mom, sank down beside her and wrapped his arm around her. Then he spoke to the officer. "Our daughter, Lynnie, is three. She would never go outside into the dark on her own."

"Tell us again where you were last night," the policeman demanded in a not-so-nice voice.

"I worked late, preparing a brief."

"Until five a.m.?"

"Yes, until five a.m. As I told you, I always check the girls' rooms before turning in. Lynnie wasn't in her bed. I woke my wife. We looked through the whole house and then we called you."

Clare had been sleeping in her brand new room. They'd moved in here—she studied her hand and counted her fingers—five days ago. Boxes were still stacked down here and upstairs. The house was okay. There were more rooms for her and Lynnie to play hide and seek. But she didn't like being alone in her own room at night. She'd liked it better when she and Lynnie had slept in the same room.

Earlier she'd thought she'd heard Lynnie's door open…thought her sister was going to the bathroom and might come in and crawl into bed with her. But she'd been *so* sleepy. She and Lynnie had been running through the hose sprayer all afternoon in the backyard while Mommy unpacked. She was supposed to watch her sister. She was always supposed to look out for Lynnie. That's what big sisters did.

Where had Lynnie gone?

Then Clare remembered the blue car that had driven down the alley in back of the yard lots of times. The man had stopped once and watched them. But she'd thought he might be one of their new neighbors who just wanted to say hi.

Should she tell the policeman?

He was so big, and he looked mad. Her dad looked mad, too, as he asked, "Why do you want to question me and my wife separately?"

"That's just the way we do it, Mr. Thaddeus."

Although she was scared of the two big men in blue uniforms, she knew her mommy and daddy wouldn't let them hurt her. Policemen helped, didn't they? They were going to help find Lynnie.

She slipped off of the chair, went over to the sofa and tugged on her mother's arm. "Mommy, when I was playing—"

The doorbell rang.

"Are you expecting someone?" the policeman asked, his brows arched.

Not sounding at all like herself, her mother answered, "I called a friend."

"Before or after you called us?"

Her mother's face turned red. "*After*, of course."

"Mommy." She tugged on her mother's arm again while one of the policemen went to the door.

Her mother took Clare's hand. "Not now, honey. Natalie's going to take care of you for a little while so we can talk to the officers."

"But, Mommy—"

Her mom's best friend, Natalie Barlow, rushed into the living room looking as upset as her mom and dad. "What can I do?"

Her father answered quickly. "Can you take Clare upstairs? And can you call our old neighbors? Maybe they'll help search. I've got to get out there looking, but I have to finish answering questions first."

Natalie gave Clare a weak smile and took her hand. "Come on, honey. Let's go upstairs for a while."

Her mom kissed her.

Her dad gave her a nod.

She tried again. "When I was playing with Lynnie—"

Tears fell down her mom's cheeks. Her dad said, "Not now. Go upstairs with Natalie."

What she had to say wasn't important. The man in the blue car didn't matter. Only Lynnie mattered.

As Clare followed Natalie upstairs, she got very afraid. What if the policemen couldn't find Lynnie? Is that why her mommy was crying? Because she didn't think they could? Was that why her dad was mad?

Natalie bent down to her. "I don't want you to worry. Everything's going to be all right."

But Clare knew better. If Lynnie didn't come home, nothing would ever be right again.

Chapter One

"**I**'m not taking it back. I bought it with my own money." Shara Thaddeus stared at her mother defiantly, standing her ground. At sixteen, she was Clare's payback for the trouble Clare had given her parents when <u>she</u> was sixteen, though certainly not for the same reason.

At thirty-two and a single parent, Clare didn't know what to do with Shara any more than her parents had known what to do with her. She'd rebelled because she'd wanted their attention. *Any* of their attention. All of their attention. When Lynnie had been around, Clare had loved her and protected her and been her big sister. But after she'd disappeared, it was as if Clare hadn't existed. Everything was always about Lynnie. And Clare had just wanted her parents to realize that although her sister was gone, *she* was still there.

Shara, on the other hand, had always had all of Clare's attention. What she didn't have was a father. She'd been a precocious child, constantly testing her boundaries. Sometimes Clare just got weary of being a watchdog. But yet wasn't that what parents were supposed to do?

After taking a deep breath for patience then putting her chin-length brown hair behind her ears, she reached out and took the blouse from Shara's hands. It really wasn't a blouse, just a stretch lace concoction that *her* daughter wasn't going to be caught dead in. "If you wear this out on the street, you'll get arrested. What did you buy to go with it?" She meant to keep her tone curious but it sounded judgmental anyway.

Shara produced a pair of black leather shorts that Clare suspected would fit too snugly.

"The outfit goes back. It's not appropriate for school. It's not appropriate to wear to the mall. It's not appropriate to be caught dusting the house in. What were you thinking?"

"I'm thinking there are a few boys who would think I'm hot."

Counting to ten had never been a strategy that worked well for Clare, especially when her daughter was deliberately trying to push her buttons. But she tried it again, nonetheless, not meeting with any more success than she'd achieved the last time. She prayed for patience, or wisdom or anything that would help deal with her daughter.

Finally, in a friendly tone she asked, "Care to give me their names? Maybe I can do background checks."

Shara studied her mother, trying to decide if she was joking or serious. "Brad said he likes me in black."

"Brad doesn't need to like you in anything. He's a

senior. You're a sophomore. We've talked about this, Shara. He has a reputation and I don't want him giving *you* a reputation."

"You are wound *so* tight," Shara mumbled.

Before Clare could deal with *that* assessment, the telephone rang. She glanced at it, thought about letting it ring, letting the answering machine take over. But maybe both she and her daughter needed a few minutes to cool down. She saw from the Caller ID that it was her mom's home number. This would probably be a short conversation. They never had much to say to each other.

Clare watched Shara take the new outfit and her other bags to her room. "They go back," Clare called after her.

Her daughter didn't bother to reply.

Clare greeted her mom with a chipper "hello," wondering what she was going to put together for supper. As an X-ray technician at the hospital, she usually arrived home after Shara. Today, however, Shara had asked her if she could stop at the mall for an hour or so after school and Clare had agreed. It looked as if they'd both be taking a trip after supper to return Shara's purchases. Maybe they should just leave now and grab pizza there. The mall on an October Friday night would be busy.

"Clare?"

The tiny crack in her mother's voice made Clare pull in a breath. "What's wrong? Has something happened to Dad?"

Although her father and mother had divorced two

years after Lynnie had disappeared, Clare had desperately tried to hold onto bonds with both of them.

"I haven't heard from your father in weeks. The last time I saw him was at the picnic you had Labor Day weekend."

It was really strange. Her parents had once had a good marriage until Lynnie was taken. Now they were awkward together whenever they had to be in the same room. Clare always felt as if she were the cause of that awkwardness, always felt as if she should do something to make it all better, always felt as if she was the neutral territory in the middle of a decades-old war.

After a short pause, her mother explained, "Detective Grove called me. He already spoke to your father."

Clare's heart skipped a beat. "Detective Grove?" The picture of a tall lean man in a rumpled suit flashed in her mind—the man who had taken over Lynnie's investigation after the patrol officers' first visit.

"Do you remember him?" her mother asked gently—too gently—and Clare had a shivery premonition of what could be coming.

"Didn't he retire?" she asked her mom, her heart racing now.

"Yes, he did. But he's not really keen on retirement and he's been…working a few cold cases." Her mother's voice was edgier than usual and a little wobbly, too.

"What are you trying to tell me, Mom?" Clare's hands became sweaty as she thought about all the possibilities. Lynnie's face at three and a half was still so vivid in her mind—the face they'd used on posters…the face she'd envisioned floating in a river…the face on the body in nightmares that had been buried in a ditch. The *not* knowing had always been worse than knowing. The not knowing is what had torn them all apart. Clare really believed that if the police had found Lynnie's body somewhere, maybe they could have gone on as a family.

Maybe.

"He wants to meet with us tomorrow morning. You, me and your dad. He thinks he has a lead."

Clare's throat went desert dry. Even though she'd only been five, she remembered the hope that had filled her parents' faces whenever a new lead had been phoned in, whenever the police had gotten a tip from an informer on the street, whenever there was a chance that Lynnie might have been spotted. She also remembered the expression on their faces when all those hopes had been dashed and one day had turned into the next without teaching them anything new.

Except that they were losing each other, hour by hour, day by day, week by week.

"What kind of lead?" Clare asked, trying to control the shakiness in her voice.

"He wouldn't tell me over the phone. He's working out of his home, so I offered the use of my office at *Yesteryear*. Can you be there tomorrow at ten?"

Her father wouldn't like meeting at her mother's shop. Now and then he'd complained to Clare that her mother was lost in the past. He didn't like the mustiness of the store or what the old furniture represented—a history that couldn't be changed…a child who would never come home. Her mother didn't see it that way at all. Her mother liked to relive every memory she had. She wrapped herself in the reminiscence of what she told Clare were the happiest years of her life. More than that, *Yesteryear* had given her a reason to get up each day, a reason to search for old furniture if not for her daughter, though Clare suspected she still looked for Lynnie everywhere she went.

Trying to prepare herself for the meeting, she shored up her courage and asked, "Did Detective Grove say whether this lead means Lynnie's alive or dead?"

A sharp intake of breath met her question and then her mom answered, "He didn't say, and I didn't ask. I still have hope, Clare. I always have."

Yes, her mother had held onto the hope that Lynnie was still alive, that some misguided woman had taken her and raised her for her own. But a misguided woman didn't steal a child from someone's house in the middle of the night.

False hope was worse than no hope at all. Clare and her dad understood each other on that one point, at least.

"I'll be there tomorrow, Mom, but please don't—" She wasn't sure how to say it.

"Please don't believe in the best rather than the worst? Oh, Clare. Maybe as you get older you'll learn that believing in the best is the only way to get through some days. I'll see you in the morning, honey."

Clare and her mother weren't on the same wavelength...would never be on the same wavelength. Just like her and Shara?

She said goodbye, hung up the phone and went to

her daughter's room. Arguing with Shara would postpone thinking about the meeting tomorrow morning…a meeting that could shake up all of their lives once more.

ABOUT THE AUTHOR

Karen Rose Smith

Award-winning author Karen Rose Smith was born in Pennsylvania. Although she was an only child, she remembers the bonds of an extended family. Since her father came from a family of ten and her mother, a family of seven, there were always aunts, uncles and cousins visiting on weekends. Family is a strong theme in her books and she suspects her childhood memories are the reason.

In college, Karen began writing poetry and also met her husband to be. They both began married life as teachers, but when their son was born, Karen decided to try her hand at a home-decorating business. She returned to teaching for a while but changes in her life led her to writing romance fiction. Now she writes romances and mysteries full time. She has sold over 80 novels since 1991.

Presently, she is hard at work on a series for Harlequin Special Edition as well as the Caprice De Luca home stager mystery series for Kensington Books.

When she isn't writing, she cares for three rescue cats, gardens, and cooks. Married to her college sweetheart since 1971, believing in the power of love and commitment, she envisions herself writing relationship novels, both romance and mystery, for a long time to come!

www.ingramcontent.com/pod-product-compliance
Lightning Source LLC
Chambersburg PA
CBHW030914120626
46554CB00001B/139